Any and All Publishing Rights
to Yucky Papas Bedtime Stories

And

Yucky Papa Trademark

Are owned by Yucky Papa Ink

Also known as Richard G
Sweitzer

Table Of Contents

LIST OF STORY CHARACTERS

CANDY-Farmer's daughter
ZEGE-   Villian
CLYDE- Boyfriend
ANN-   Associate
BENNY-Muscle
JOE -   Muscle
TONY-   Candy's lover
ETHEL- Stable boss

From farmer's daughter to crime boss.
Follow the adventures of how she makes her way to the top.

Candy

Grampa Boyd was a rich farmer, who owned a large farm in Ohio. He had an attractive daughter, Hellen, who was full of energy and spirit. She was happy and always curious about what was going on around her, and about life in general.

Hellen was 16 years old and loved living on her father's farms. Each day she looked forward to helping on the farm by taking care of the animals and collective the eggs in the hen house.

After the morning chores, Hellen and her mom and dad sat down to a large breakfast of eggs, ham or bacon, fresh fried potatoes, milk, and fruit, all of which was produced on the farm. After breakfast Hellen took a shower, got dressed, and went to school. She was a good student and enjoyed school. She always made good grades. While Hellen was in school, her mother baked fresh bread and cake and pies. Mom also canned fruits and vegetables grown on the farm. Father and his two immigrant farm hands did the daily chores on the farm. The farm hands were Clyde and his father. When Hellen came home from school, she liked to spend time with Clyde. He was 30 years old. As time went by, Hellen and Clyde became romantically involved. The day came when Hellen began to get sick in the morning. Hellen's mother took her to the doctor. After the doctor examined Hellen, he told them Hellen was pregnant. She began to cry. She knew her father would be angry. Mom asked Hellen who the father was and said they'd have to tell her father "and you know he'll be angry."

"Clyde is the father", answered Hellen still crying.

"Are you talking about the farm hand Clyde?" Her mother asked.

"yes." said Hellen.

"Your father will definitely be angry, and Clyde will most likely lose his job on the farm," said her mom.

Hellen was a scared, confused 16 years old who was uncertain about her future. Her mom tried to comfort her as they drove home from the doctor. When Hellen and her mom got home, her mom told her to go get Clyde and bring him to the house. "Have him wait on the porch while I talk to your father."

"OK," said Hellen and she went to get Clyde. As Hellen and Clyde approached the house, they could hear her father ranting and angrily yelling curses. "I will not have a bastard in my home. I'll have the SOB put in jail. I'll kill him, the SOB."

The more her mom tried to calm her father, the angrier he got. Hearing the commotion in the house, Clyde told Hellen, "There's no way I'm staying here."

Hellen asked him if he was going to run out on her. He told her no. "If you want to come with me, you can."

At that, Hellen took Clyde's hand and two of them quickly walked toward the farm hands' house. As they approached the farm hands' house, they saw Clyde's father sitting on the porch in a rocking chair. Clyde and his father had a conversation in Spanish. His father went into the house. After a short time, he came back out, said something to Clyde, and handed him keys and some money. He gave Clyde a big hug and small suit case.

"What's going on?" Asked Hellen, "Are we going somewhere?

"My father gave me five hundred dollars and the keys to the truck," he told her. "He also suggested we leave here immediately."

As they got in the truck, Hellen saw her father walking toward them. Hellen knew she would never see her mother and father again. As the truck left the farm, she began to cry. She would miss the farm, her parents, and her friends at school. As they traveled down the road, both saying little for what seemed like forever, Clyde said, "We need gas. I'm hungry. How about you?"

"Me too," replied Hellen.

They pulled into a truck stop parking lot and went inside. The truck stop was your typical stop with gas pumps, bus stops, and a restaurant. As they sat at their table, not saying too much, Clyde said, "I need some coffee, What do you want Hellen?"

"Hot chocolate sounds good, and something to eat," said Hellen. "Where are we going?" asked Hellen

The waitress came to the table and took the order. "I'll be right back with your drinks," she said and walked away.

"You know, Clyde, I'm hungry, tired, scared, a little sick, and you still haven't told me where we're going," she said.

The waitress brought their drinks and told them their order would be up soon and walked away. Clyde sat quietly drinking his coffee. Hellen too. The waitress served them their food and asked if they wanted something else. They replied, "Thank you, no," and the waitress left the table. Hellen looked up from her food and looked Clyde in the eyes and said, "You still haven't answered my question. Where are we going?"

Clyde looked up. Hellen was looking at him with a serious, stern look on her face. He knew he had to answer her Questions. "My father had a suggestion," said Clyde. "Maybe you get an abortion. He gave me the money to pay for it."

"I feel sick," Hellen said as she ran for the bathroom. After vomiting, she stood in the bathroom looking in the mirror crying. After regaining her composure, she went back to the table. "I don't want an abortion," she said.

"OK with me," he said, "We will work it out somehow.

She was relieved. When done eating and paying the check, Clyde put gas in the truck and they left the truck stop. As they traveled the high way, Hellen asked again, "So where are we going?

"I'm thinking Chicago," replied Clyde. "Have you been there before?"

"No," she answered. "What's in Chicago?"

"The streets are paved in gold."

"You're exaggerating, right?" she replied.

"A little bit," he said, "but there is money there to be made.

Hellen was feeling comforted about the future. If she knew what Clyde was really thinking, she would have been terrified. She fell asleep. When she woke up, it was still daylight. She could see big buildings and signs saying, "Welcome to Chicago." The traffic was heavy. Coming from a small town, Hellen was in awe. "Where we at," She asked.

"We're on Shroring Park BLVD heading to Broadway Street," he replied. "Money and cheap housing," he added.

At Broadway and Irvine Parkway they stopped for breakfast at a diner. After the waitress taken their order and brought their food, Clyde asked her where a cheap hotel was. "About a block down in the shamrock. They rent by the day or week," she answered.

After breakfast, they drove to the hotel. They could see Wriggly field from the hotel parking lot. The clerk asked them if they wanted to rent by the hour, day, or week.

Hellen laughed, "Do people really rent rooms by the hour?"

"All the time," the clerk answered

"We'd like a room by the week," Clyde said.

"That will be forty-five dollars and a ten dollar key deposit," said the clerk.

"We'll take it," said Clyde.

After paying, the clerk told them to take the elevator to the third floor. The room was small. It had a bed and dresser. The bathroom was down the hall. So was the pay phone. "I'm going to check a couple of things. You stay here. I'll be back soon," he said and left her in the room.

Hellen looked out the dirty window. The room left a lot to be desired. She wondered why the women were standing by curbs and talking to the people in the cars driving by. From time to time they'd get in the cars. She began to wonder when Clyde was coming back. He was gone a long time. Had he taken off and left her? Suddenly, she felt alone and scared. He wouldn't do that, she told herself. The more time that passed, the more upset she got. At the point of panic, she heard a key in the door. As the door opened, Clyde entered the room. Hellen was relieved. She ran to Clyde and threw her arms around him.

"Why you so emotional?" he asked.

"I'm OK," She said. "Just being silly."

They worked their way to the bed and made love. Hellen fell asleep in Clyde's arms. She felt safe. She woke up early the next morning. The room was very hot, making sleep difficult. She went to the public bath to take a shower. When she got back to the room, Clyde was talking to two women. "Hello. This is Miss Ruby and her employee Gigi. We now work for Miss Ruby," said Clyde with a big smile.

"She's everything you said," said Miss Ruby. "I believe we agreed on two thousand?"

"Yes, Mama. Two thousand," said Clyde.

"What's going on?" asked Hellen. "What's the two thousand for?"

"Miss Ruby will explain it all to you," said Clyde.

"Take this note to the Red Slipper and ask for Reggie," said Gigi to Clyde. With that, Clyde left.

"Is that all the clothes you have?" asked Ruby.

"Yes," said Hellen.

"Gigi, take Hellen and get her some clothes. See you at the apartment."

Clyde waked in the Red Slipper. There was a large man behind the bar. "Where would I find Reggie?" asked Clyde.

"who wants to know?" he asked back.

"Ruby told me to give this note to Reggie."

"I'm Reggie," said the man.

Clyde handed him the note. "Come with me," the man said to Clyde. The two went into a back room. "Have a seat," the man said. "Did Ruby pay you?"

"Yes," said Clyde. The man walked behind Clyde sitting in the chair, took out a gun, and shot Clyde in the head. He was dead. The man took the money off Clyde's body and called for a couple of men to come to the back room. "Take out the trash and clean up the room," he told them, and went back to the bar.

By now Hellen and Gigi were at Ruby's apartment. There were eight other woman at the apartment. "Ladies, this is Candy," Gigi told the women.

"My name is Hellen," she said.

"From now on, honey, your name is Candy," she said as she walked up to Hellen with a menacing look on her face. "You're not going to give me a problem right off, Are you?"

"I don't like this," Hellen said. "I need to talk to Clyde. Where is Clyde?"

"He's history," said Gigi. "Ladies, show Candy the ropes. Help her learn the rules." With that, two of the women took Candy by the arms and took her into one of the bedrooms. Gigi prepared a syringe and joined the three women in the bedroom. Candy was sitting on the bed naked. "You'll be a good earner," said Gigi as she approached the bed next to Candy. "Spread your legs," ordered Gigi. Candy refused. "Help her," she told the two women, and they did. Gigi emptied the syringe into Candy's genital area. Seconds later, Candy was totally stoned. "Yes mama, Candy, you'll defiantly be a good earner." She could hear Gigi talking. It was like she'd left her body. The three workers left the room. Candy lay on the bed dazed and naked. Hours later, Candy came out of the bedroom still dazed and naked. Her vision was blurred.

"How you feeling?" a worker asked. She was having a problem focusing and understanding. Another voice said, "Let's take her into the bathroom and clean her up. She's vomited on herself." They put her in the shower and started washing her. As they washed Candy, she found herself experiencing sexual pleasure as the two massaged her breasts and genitals and rectum. After bathing her, they took her to the bed and continued having their way with her. As Candy came down from her high, she began returning their sexual favors. She felt penetration of a hard object in the genitals. It felt good. She gave one of the women oral sex. While, being penetrated by the hard object in her genitals and rectum, it was like no experience she'd ever had before. After they finished, the two women asked her how she felt.

"I never felt like this in my life," she answered.

The three women got dressed and went into the living room. Ruby suggested they go have something to eat, and they did. As Candy sat in the restaurant, her genitals and rectum were still feeling good. After dinner, they went to the Red Slipper. The women sat at a table. A waitress came to the table. "Your usual Ruby and Gigi?"

"Yes," said the women. "Bring Candy a vodka, neat."

There were women dancing on the stage while taking off their clothes. "How can women do that?" Candy asked.

"Honey, in a few short days, you'll be doing the same and more," said Ruby.

"Not me," said Candy.

"We'll see," said Gigi.

Reggie came to the table and gave Ruby a lot of cash.

"Has the trach been taken out," she asked Reggie.

"Yes," he answered. "Is this the new talent?"

"Yes," said Ruby. "In fact, there's no time like the present to start her training. Go with Reggie," Ruby told Candy. "Reggie is a large man with a lot of body hair."

"I'm afraid," said Candy.

"Here honey, take this vitamin." and candy did.

"Feel better," asked Ruby.

"Yes," said Candy.

Reggie led Candy by the hand to the back room. Reggie used every opening Cany had. Afterward Reggie told Candy to go on stage and perform. And she did. All Candy knew is that she felt good. A few hours later, Reggie closed up the bar and took Candy to Ruby's apartment.

"How'd she do?" Gigi asked.

"She's a natural," Reggie said.

"Candy, why don't you go to bed and get some sleep," said Ruby. And she did.

After sleeping a few hours, Candy woke up. The drugs had worn off. Her genitals and rectum hurt big time. She started to cry. Where did Clyde go? Would she ever see him again? What had she done that day. How would the days events affect her baby? Gigi came into the room.

"I heard you crying. Are you OK, honey?" she asked Candy.

"No," said Candy. "My genitals and rectum hurt big time. Where's Clyde. Why can't I see and talk to him."

"Clyde's gone forever. Forget him," said Gigi. "Take this. It'll make the pain go away."

"Not this time," said Candy. "I want Clyde. I want to go home."

Gigi left the room. Moments later she returned with another woman. "Pull your panties down and spread your legs," Gigi told her.

"No," said Candy. "No way."

The women left the room and came back moments later with another woman. Two of the women held her down and spread her legs. Gigi emptied a syringe by her genitals. Seconds later, Candy was once again stoned. Late into the next day, Candy woke up still kind of hazy. one of the girls was sitting next to the bed. When Candy started to move about and speak, the girl told her to "take it easy, Honey," and left the room. Moments later the girl and Gigi came back into the room.

"You OK, honey?" asked Gigi.

"I'm hungry and thirsty," said Candy.

"We'll get you something to eat and coffee," Gigi told her. "Why don't you take a shower and get dressed?"

"OK," said Candy.

When she was done taking a shower and getting dressed, there was a tray of food an coffee waiting for her. Gigi had left the room. The girl was still there.

"You feel better now, honey?" she asked. "eat your meal and wake up some. You know, I used to feel the way you do. Believe me, the more you resist, the worse it gets. Resist long enough, they will just kill you."

"I'm pregnant," Candy told the girl. "I don't want to hurt my baby.

"Damn honey. Why did you keep it a secret. Ruby would help you out. I'll get Ruby for you." And the girl left the room. For the first time in days, Candy had hope. Ruby came in the room.

"Is it true you're pregnant, Candy?" she asked. "How far along are you?"

"I think about five weeks," Candy answered.

"You stay here and rest. I'll have a doctor here in less than an hour," said Ruby.

With tender loving since, Candy was feeling a lot better. An hour later Ruby, Gigi, Reggie, a forth girl, and a heavy set man with a wrinkled shirt came into the room. He had dirty finger nails, rotten teeth, and was unshaven. "This is doctor Stanly. He's going to examine you," said Ruby with a smile.

"Maybe he should wash his hands first," Candy said concerned.

The doctor took off his coat. "Have you got a clothes hanger? I'm going to give you something to relax you, OK?" he asked.

"I guess," Candy replied.

"Here, take this and relax." A few moments after taking the pill, Candy felt light headed. She could hear them talking, but could not understand them. Candy could feel her pants and underpants being pulled off.

"What's going on?" Candy asked.

"Relax, honey. The Doctor said it'll be over soon."

Candy could see the doctor unbending the clothes hanger. She knew this wasn't good. "What are you going to do with that?" Candy asked.

"It might hurt a little. It'll be over soon.

Candy could feel something sharp inside her. "Stop. What are you doing? You'll kill my baby!" she screamed.

"Hold her down," the doctor said. The four of them held her down. Candy could feel warm fluid running on her butt. Finally she passed out. When Candy woke up, she felt something between her legs. She reached down. There were two wet kotex by her genitals. When she brought her hand up by her face, there was blood on them. Candy screamed. One of the girls came into the room. She had more kotex. She removed the bloody kotex and put a fresh one on her.

"What did they do to me?" Candy demanded to know.

"They helped you deal with your pregnancy."

"What's that mean?" Candy asked.

"You're not pregnant anymore," the girl said.

"They killed my baby? They killed my baby? How could they kill my baby?"

Gigi came into the room. She had a syringe in her hand. "No. No," screamed Candy. "You killed my baby."

The girl held Candy's arms while Gigi emptied the syringe in her. Candy passed out. Five days later, Candy woke up. She felt between her legs. The kotex were gone. She had stopped bleeding. A girl sitting in the room saw she was awake. "We didn't know if you were going to make it," she told Candy. "How are you feeling? Do you have any pain?"

"No," replied Candy. "I am hungry."

"I'll get you something to eat." And she left the room. A few moments later, Ruby came into the room.

"I'm glad you're OK,"

Candy couldn't say anything. She began to recall what Ruby, Gigi, the doctor, and Reggie had done to her. She smiled. "How long have I been asleep?" she asked Ruby.

"Five days," replied Ruby. "How you feeling?"

"I feel good," she answered. "Thank you for helping me with my pregnancy. I promise I'll be the best earner you ever saw.

"I'm sure you will," replied Ruby. "You rest today. Tomorrow you start back to work. OK?"

"OK," said Candy as she smiled.

Ruby left the room. Candy knew in her mind and heart the day would come when she would return the kindness Ruby, Gigi, Reggie and the two girls had shown her when they killed her baby. After a month, Ruby moved Candy to the hundred dollar room and raised her percentage to twenty after the first five hundred. As time passed, Candy gained Ruby, Gigi, and Regie's trust. They began grooming her for management. They even trusted her with the safe combination. She no longer had to dance on stage. She had her own special clients. She eventually befriended two men, Benny and Joe. They were both large men. She would occasionally give them freebies for doing her bidding. As time passed, Candy Benny and Joe grew very close. When the day came, they would play an important part in returning Ruby and the others' kindness.

Days turned into weeks and months. The seasons came and went. One day Candy started quietly talking to other girls, except for the two that helped kill her baby, as well as the women that worked for the other pimps. She promised them if she got control, they'd get to keep forty percent of their daily income. They gladly agreed to help her. She impressed on them that secrecy was most important. The day came for Candy to make her move. Candy had Benny and Joe's brothers in. The two were large men, anxious to make money, and could keep their mouths shut.

That night, at the bar, she told Benny and Joe, "Tomorrow." And when they saw Reggie leave the bar with a bottle of champagne, they should come to the apartment, wait outside the apartment door until she let them in. "And be quiet. Bring your brothers with you. Be sober."

That night, Candy told Ruby and Gigi she wanted to show her thanks and gratitude for all they did for her. Tomorrow, she also asked if Mimi and Debbie could be there. she would give them all the sex they ever had and maybe Reggie could come. "I can't wait to feel his large member in me." And if he could bring a bottle of champagne with him.

"I'd like that," Said Ruby. Gigi said the same.

That night, Candy, Ruby, and Gigi slept in the same bed naked. Candy went to sleep knowing tomorrow she'd take care of business. The next day, Candy put on see through baby doll nighty, and no panties, and went to the bar. "Aren't you ladies overdressed?" said Candy.

"You know, you're right." They replied.

"Why you hiding your big tasty member?" asked Candy of Reggie. He quickly removed his clothes. "I like invited a couple of clients. They both have large members. They should be here shortly. Your member looks delicious," Candy told Reggie. "I can't wait to feel it inside me. Where's the champagne?" Candy went on.

Reggie handed Candy the bottle. "You folks start warming up while I pour the drinks." As Candy poured the drinks, Benny and Joe arrived. Gigi let them in.

"I hear you boys have large members," said Ruby.

"Yes, Ma'am," they answered.

"Don't stand there with your clothes on. Let's see what you got." The men took off their clothes. They were very large. "We like," the women exclaimed.

After Candy filled the glasses, she put ground up pills in Ruby, Gigi, Mimi, Debbie, and Regie's glasses. She passed out the drinks to the all. " A toast to hot genitalia and large members." they all drank all of their drinks in one gulp.

"Let's get started," said Ruby. "I'm already wet."

"I second that," said Gigi.

Moments later Ruby, Gigi, Reggie, Mimi, and Debbie were all but unconscious.

Candy told Bennie and Joe, "You know what to do."

They both put on their clothes, took out two large knives, and slit the women from their genitals to their belly buttons.

"I'll take care of Reggie," Candy said.

She stroked Reggie until he got hard, took a knife, cut his member off below his testicles, stuffed it in his mouth, and held her hand over his mouth until he choked to death.

"I believe I have repaid their kindness," Candy said. "May they rot in hell!"

She opened the door. Bennie and Joe's brothers were waiting there.

"Take out the trash after you take their money, and clean up the room. When you are done, come to the bar."

With that, Candy, Bennie, and Joe left for the bar. On the way to the bar, Candy asked if the flyers got handed out.

"Yes," said the men.

So far, so good. When they got to the bar, Candy told the men to come in the back door and wait in the back room until they were needed. Candy walked up to the two bouncers and told them she wanted to feel their members in her and she would do both of them as she rubbed their groin area. The men were getting hard.

"What say fellas? How about we go in the back room and have a good time?"

"Sounds good," they said.

Candy walked to the back room, a man on each arm. As the three entered the back room, they saw Benny and Joe with guns with silencers.

"Come in gentlemen and have a seat," Candy told them. "When you are done, take out the trash and clean the room."

Candy left the room, shut the door behind her. The two brothers were there.

"Go to the back room and help Bennie and Joe." They did.

The bar was jumping. All the women were making money. Candy made herself a drink. It was all coming together. She went to the back and told Benny to come and tend bar. As she and Benny sat and talked, Candy said, "I need to be alone for a few moments," and went into the bathroom where she cried for a short time. She wished she could kill the people that killed her man and baby again and again.

The door opened up a little. "You OK," Bennie asked.

"I'm OK. I'll be out in a moment."

She left the bathroom and went to finish her drink.

"Give me another one," she said.

"Not too much," Bennie said. "You have to keep your wits about you."

Joe and the two brothers came into the bar. " The trash is out and the rooms are clean," said Joe.

"Good job," Candy replied. "Have a seat, a drink, and relax for a while. What time is it?"

"About two PM," Joe answered.

"Anybody hungry besides me?" she asked.

All of the men said that they could eat.

"Lunch is on me," she said. "Joe, you and your brother mind the bar. What do you want me to bring back for you for lunch?"

She wrote down the order. The three left. At the restaurant, Candy talked about the party tonight.

"If we close the bar early, it might raise suspicion. Therefore, we have to prepare for the party while the bar is open. I want set up an executive section just for the pimps. I don't want any of the working girls in that section. If you're wondering why, I spent a lot of money on an imported booze for them tonight. The brothers marked it x. It's for the pimps only. I figure the final step should be to complete in the first fifteen minutes of the party. After that, all that's left is taking out trash, and the women will be more than glad to help. Until the last step happens, I want the pimps treated like royalty. OK, guys?"

"Sure thing, Candy," the men said.

"We should get back. Joe and his brother are probably real hungry."

After getting Joe and his brother's food, they went back to the bar. When they got back to the bar, Candy told the men, "one of you needs to stay and tend bar, the other three can take off till six PM."

"I'll stay," volunteered Joe's brother.

"fine by me," replied Candy. "Remember be back by six sober and ready to take care of business." The three men left. "All you have to do is tend bar and watch over the women."

Candy made herself a drink and went into the back room. As she sat at her desk making preparation for the party, Joes brother came into the office.

"The way I look at it, you owe me. You owe me big time."

"I don't understand. Do I owe you money or what?" Candy asked.

"You have banged Benny and Joe many times. I do as much for you as they do, so it's time it's my turn, one way or another."

"You know you're right. How do you like it? Oral, front, back, what's your pleasure?" asked Candy.

"All three," he answered.

"Let's go to the hundred dollar room. We'll be more comfortable there, OK?"

"OK," he said.

In the room, Candy picked a cloth bag.

"What's in there?" he asked. "I'm wise to your tricks."

"Won't you at least allow me to use lubricant if you want back door?"

"I guess that's reasonable," he said.

"Come on honey, take off your clothes. You can't get laid with your pants on," she said.

"You first," he demanded."

"How about at the same time," she replied.

"OK," he said. "Don't you laugh at me. If you laugh at me, I'll kill you."

"Are you kidding me? I can't wait to have your member in me," she said as she started getting undressed. "It's your turn," she told him as she stood in her bra and panties in front of him.

As he took his shirt and pants off, she saw his member was very big and hard. She finished undressing and laid on the bed.

"Take your shorts off and bring that luscious member to me," Candy said as she opened her legs.

He jammed his member in her.

"It hurts, she said.

"Not my problem. You should be used to it," as he continued to penetrate her. Fortunately, it didn't last very long.

"Umm, that was great. I haven't had sex that good in a long time," Candy said. She hoped he believed her. If he didn't, she was dead. "Can I lick it clean for you?" she asked as she sat up on the bed.

"Sure. That would be great," he answered. She did.

After a few minutes, Candy said, "You know, it's getting late. We have to get back to work.

"No hard feelings?" he asked.

"No way," she said. "I'd like to do it again soon.

She left the hundred dollar room, went to the bar, and got a drink. He came up to the bar.

"I can use a cold beer," he said.

"Help yourself," Candy said and finished her drink. It was six PM. Where were Benny, Joe, and Benny's brother? Candy was trying to decide how to deal with Joe's brother. If it were anybody else, she'd just kill them. He was behind the bar. He was staring at her. She gave him a big smile. She had to keep him at ease until the other men got there. Where were they? A few moments later, the three men finally came in the bar.

"Sorry we're late. It took a little while to find the right truck."

"Joe, go in the back room and get the booze for the pimps ready for tonight. Benny, you stay with me. You two brothers, have a seat at the bar and watch over the women. OK?" Candy asked.

"Sure thing," they answered and they did.

That night, everything went as planned. Candy noticed a well-dressed man sitting with the women instead of with the pimps. Candy walked up to him.

"Hi handsome. Having a good time? I'm Candy," she said.

"I'm Ruby's lawyer. I'm here to make sure her interests are taken care of," he said

"I'm certain if I didn't give you the royal treatment, Ruby would have my ass. We don't want that, do we?" stated Candy with a big smile. Won't you let pleasure you, please."

"Why not," he said.

"Come with me to the best room in the house," she said as she took him by the arm and went into the hundred dollar room.

Candy closed the door behind them. "Take a seat. Get comfortable," she told him. He did. "I'll start with a strip tease dance," she said. "I'll just find some music on the radio. As she turned on the radio, she took a gun with a silencer from the drawer. Are you ready honey?" she asked with her back to him.

"Bring it on, baby," he replied.

Candy turned and faced him holding the gun on him. "Now don't move or get out of the chair. I don't want to shoot you," she said. "We're going to play a game. I'm going to say something and you have to repeat it word for word. If you don't, you might make me do something you'll regret. Okay?" Candy explained.

"You got my attention," he answered.

"Repeat after me. I'm a dirt bag lawyer that prays on young, innocent women for profit," candy told him.

"Ruby won't like this at all," he said.

Candy shot him in both knees.

"Now you see, you've gone and made me do something you regret."

"You're crazy, bitch," He blurted out holding his knees.

The room door opened. "Pardon the intrusion. Just wanted to let you know it's all over. The men are taking out the trash now with the women's help," said Joe.

"Thank you," replied Candy. "When you are done with the trash, get the trash in here too."

"Okay," said Joe and closed the door.

She turned her attention back to the lawyer. "How you doing?" she asked him.

"I'm in a lot of pain. How do you think I'm doing, you crazy bitch?" he said.

Candy shot him in both legs very close to his member.

"Now you see, you went and made me do something you regret," she said with a big smile. "Repeat after me. I am a dirt bag lawyer that prays on innocent, young women for profit, and I deserve to be dead."

"You bitch. You'd better kill me. If you don't, Ruby is going to do a number on you," he said in great pain.

She shot him in his member. "You did it again. You've got to stop making me do things you regret," she said with a big grin on her face.

"You crazy bitch," he blurted out holding his member with both hands in great pain.

She shot him in the chest. He was dead.

Candy grabbed him by his hair, put the gun in his mouth, and pulled the trigger. That's one less dirt bag in the world, she thought as she put the gun away and went back to the bar room.

All of the trash was gone in the bar. Benny and Joe and the brothers were standing by the bar.

"Two of you, get the trash in the hundred dollar room, clean up any mess, and dispose of it," she ordered. They did.

While the men disposed of the trash, Candy made brief statements to the women. She also told them the new rules. She ended by declaring, "Let's party." They all stood, clapped, cheered, and began to party.

By then, the men had returned. The two brothers tended bar. Candy waved Benny and Joe to her. "I'm going home. Let the women party for a couple of hours, make sure they're here tomorrow ready to work, send them home, and close up the bar. Good night."

Most of the night, she tossed and turned. She still had to resolve the problem with Joe's brother without creating a rift in management. She knew what had to be done. She just wasn't sure who should do it, or how.

By the time she went to the bar the next day, she had made up her mind. She would do what needed doing. During business that day she asked Joe's brother to join her in the office.

"I want you to know, I really liked our experience together last time. In fact, it was better than the front door."

He got a big smile on his face.

She went on. "I'd like to do it again tonight after work. However, it must be a secret. You can't tell anybody, not even your brother. If you do, you'll never get my rectum again. Understand?"

"Yes," he said.

"Here's what you do. You tell Joe you don't feel well and ask him if you can go home at midnight tonight. Wait a block down the street. I'll meet you there twenty minutes later. Pick up a bottle of white wine. You don't need any lube. It felt good without it. Remember, tell no one. Because if you do, you'll never have my ass again. Now get back to work."

"Okay," he said with a big smile. "Until tonight."

She winked at him and gave him a big smile. In her mind, she knew that night would bring her more pleasure than he would have.

A few minutes before midnight, she walked up to him, started rubbing his member area, and whispered in his ear. "I want the best wine the store has, Okay?"

"Okay," he answered.

As she walked to the bar, she said to herself that the man definitely had a big member. What a waste. At the bar, she ordered a drink and took it to her office. As she sat at her desk drinking and smoking a cigarette, she took a gun out of the drawer and a rag. She checked the gun to make sure it was loaded. It wasn't. She filled the clip with wand cutter bullets. She put the gun and rag in her bag and took off her panties.

As she touched herself for a few short moments, she found herself getting excited at the idea of doing Joes brother. She reached in the drawer and took out a tube of lube. Maybe she would, maybe not. She put it in her bag, went out to the bar, sat down, and finished her drink.

As she watched Joe's brother, he barely took his eyes off her. She smiled at him. He smiled back. If he's grin got any bigger, he'd explode his whole face. At midnight, he left the bar. Candy looked around the bar. She didn't see anything unusual. She waved for Benny to come to her.

"I'm calling it a night. I'm tired. Make sure to take care of business. Settle with the women and lock up. See you tomorrow."

She left. As she went to meet him, she couldn't help getting excited about doing Joe's brother. Maybe she'd do him one more time. When she met up with him, he got all grabby. She calmed him down. She made up her mind. She just wanted him dead.

"Come. Let's walk to the beach. We'll drink and get laid and have a good time," she told him.

"Sounds good to me," he replied.

"I didn't wear any panties to make it easy for you," she said as they walked to the beach.

He put his hand under her dress and played with her butt.

"Slow down, man. You'll get it very soon," she told him.

He didn't stop. She thought, what the hell. It will be over soon, besides, she was beginning to enjoy it.

As they walked she rubbed him member area. When they reached the beach, she sat down. Her dress rose up. He could see her all. He started to mount her.

"Stop. Sit down. We'll work up to that. You'll be glad you waited. Open the wine. Let's have a good time and get drunk, and then laid. Meantime, you can touch all you want," she told him. He did.

"Why do you still have your pants on? Let me see that big member."

It took about three seconds for him to take off his pants.

"That's one big member," she said.

She began stroking it.

"Lay down and close your eyes. I have a real treat for you."

"What is it?" he demanded to know.

"If you don't close your eyes, you'll never know," she said.

"I promise," he said.

She took the gun from her bag.

"Open your mouth, honey. You'll love what happens next." As she stroked his member, she said, "I want you to stroke your member and keep your eyes closed." He did.

She put the gun in his mouth and pulled the trigger. He was dead. She wiped off the gun and put it in his free hand to make it look like a suicide. As she looked to make sure everything was just so, she noticed he had climaxed. He lay dead with his member in his hand. She didn't know a dead man could cum. Candy took his money and wine. No sense in wasting it. She left the beach.

As she walked down Broadway Avenue, she felt as though a heavy weight had been lifted from her shoulders. Joe's brother was no longer a problem and there wasn't a rift in management. All was good.

She saw the Broadway Diner. The place was empty except a woman sitting at one of the tables. She went in.

"You know you can't bring the wine in here. On the other hand, if you're willing to share, take a seat," the woman said.

Candy sat at the woman's table. She got two glasses. Candy poured the wine. As they drank the wine and talked, Candy learned the woman's name was Ethel. Her man took all her money, beat her up, took her car, told her to drop dead, and left.

Her rent was due. She barely made enough to buy a pack of cigarettes and a six pack of beer on an average day, let alone pay the rent. She knew where he lived and someday she'd get even.

Ethel was a large, unattractive woman. She had whiskers and a mustache. The only thing feminine about her was that she had large breasts.

After the women drank all the wine, Candy told Ether she could fix all her problems and, if she wanted, she could get her laid.

"I have a job you're perfect for. The pay is good, it comes with an apartment, and the work is easy. You start now. When you're ready, we can pay your man a visit and give him an attitude adjustment. We'll get your money and car back."

Candy took a sheet of paper from her bag, gave Ethel the paper, and said, "Write what I say. I Quit. Put that on the register and let's start your new life."

The women went outside and hailed a cab.

"Where to ladies," the driver asked.

"Give him the address," Candy said.

Ethel gave him the address. When they got to the address, candy told the driver to wait. The women went to her man's apartment. Candy knocked on the door. She told Ethel to stand aside as not to be seen. A man came to the door. He was big. He looked and smelled like a real dirt bag. His teeth were either missing or rotted.

"What you want?" the man asked rudely.

Both women pushed their way into the apartment. Candy had taken a gun from her bag.

"Take a seat and behave and I might let you live," Candy told him. Though drunk, he sobered up fast. "It would seem you owe this lady money and the return of her car," Candy told him.

"Sure thing. Whatever you say," he said as he handed Ethel the keys.

"I'm waiting for the money you took from me. I want it now," Ethel demanded.

"It's gone," he said. "But I swear, I'll pay it back as soon as I can. Have mercy, please."

Ethel asked Candy, "Should we show him mercy?"

"Please," the man begged.

Candy shot him dead, grabbed him by the hair, put the gun in his mouth, and shot him again.

"I'm good. How about you, Ethel?" candy asked.

"I'm good," she replied.

The women went back to the street.

"You see your car?" asked Candy.

"Yes. It's parked just a ways down the street," she replied.

"You go to the car. I'll join you shortly, Candy told her as she walked up to the cab. "How much do I owe you?" she asked.

"I figure you got lots of money. Twenty dollars and a BJ for waiting all this time," he said.

"Seems fair to me," she replied as she went into her bag, pulled out her gun, and killed him dead. As she put the gun away, she said out loud, "Get greedy, get dead."

The two women got into Ethel's car and drove to Candy's place. On the way home, Candy told Ether what her job would be and that it paid a thousand cash a week and a free apartment in a good area. She'd be responsible for overseeing and watching over a little less than two hundred women. She told her that she had three rules. Never make a promise you can't keep. Always be fair. Get greedy, get dead.

Ethel spent that night al Candy's home. The next morning, they went to the bar before it opened for business. Candy told the women that they answered directly to Ethel. Ethel answered directly to Benny and Joe. All of them, if or when needed, answered to her. Never skip the chain of command.

After the meeting, Candy gave Ethel a week's pay in advance and told her to go buy some decent clothes and move into her new apartment. "Be here tomorrow ready to go to work," she told her. "It's Benny and Joe's Job to settle up with the women every day."

For the next three weeks, everything went smoothly. Candy's birthday was coming up. Each year, for her birthday, the women would give her a birthday card. She'd read each and every one. One card concerned her. It was from Ann. She was one of the women. Ann wanted to know why she and the others had to pay Ethel a fifteen percent tax on their days earnings. Candy told Ben and Joe to look into it quietly and get back to her ASAP. "Do not talk to Ethel about it. I'll do that," she told them.

A couple of days later, she called Benny and Joe and Ethel into the office. She told Ethel it was time to give her a raise for all the good work she was doing. Candy told Ethel to take a seat. She did. She was all smiles. Candy told Benny and Joe to get everyone a drink, and they did.

Candy began, "You're doing a good job keeping the women in line and resolving any problems they have, and I really appreciate it. There is one little thing I need your help dealing with. Can I count on you?"

"Absolutely," replied Ethel.

Benny and Joe moved close to Ethel with their guns in hand.

"It has come to my attention that somebody is taxing the women on their earnings. How do you think I should handle the situation? Take a minute and think about it before you answer," said Candy.

Ethel started to squirm in her chair nervously. Ethel gave no response.

"Your silence makes me think you're not telling me what you know about the problem," stated Candy. "Benny and Joe, what do you know about the problem?"

"The women tell us, if they didn't pay her a fifteen percent tax on their daily earning, she'd give them an attitude adjustment," the two men answered.

"Ethel, do you remember me telling you my three rules when I hired you?" Candy asked.

"I messed up. I'm sorry. I'll do whatever it takes to make things right," Ethel blurted out.

"You didn't answer my questions," Candy told her. "What are the three rules that I told you. I'm waiting. don't make promises you can't keep, be fair, and get greedy get dead."

The two men shot her in the back of the head. She was dead. Problem solved.

"Take out the trash, send Ann to my office after your done taking out the trash," Candy ordered.

A few minutes later, Ann came to Candy's office.

"Do you know why I called you here?" Candy asked.

"No," she replied nervously.

"The first thing you can do for me is relax. I'm promoting you to my personal assistant. It pays two thousand dollars a week, cash. You no longer have to work the stage or take care of the clients. All you have to do is take care of any and all my needs as needed. You'll live with me. Take the rest of the day off. Be back tonight around closing time for a short meeting. Any questions?" Candy asked.

"No ma'am," she replied. "And thank you."

"Enjoy your day off," Candy said with a smile.

Around closing time, Candy called the meeting to order. "Good evening, ladies and gentlemen. I have a short announcement. I won't take too much of your time. Effective immediately, Ann is my personal assistant. She answers to me only. Ethel is no longer with the company. I've repealed her fifteen percent tax."

All of the women cheered and clapped.

"I'm setting up a five person grievance committee. You ladies will nominate and vote for these persons. They will meet once a week here every Friday. Those persons will do that along with their regular duties. It pays a hundred dollars per session. They will hear and resolve any problems you ladies might have. They will answer to Benny and Joe who will review, approve, or reject the committee decision."

Candy told Benny and Joe to train Ann and the grievance committee how to deal with those who got greedy. Soon they became proficient at it. Things were going good. Her only problem was how to deal with the large amounts of money the company was bringing in.

Candy told Benny and Joe that she was taking a trip to relax and think things out. She told the two men to take care of the business, keep an eye on Ann and handle any problems the way she would.

As she sat at the table eating in the open air restaurant in Havana, a tall, dark-skinned man with long, black, wavy hair approached. He was buffed. He was an Adonis.

"It looks delicious," he said to her.

"It is," she replied.

"I wasn't talking about the food," he said.

"Neither was I," she answered.

That was the beginning of a lifelong romance and business relationship. His name was Toney. He owned several businesses on the islands. Once a month, Candy would go to the island and bring a case with millions of dollars in cash in it. Toney would launder it through his businesses. Over time, Candy had amassed a fortune worth over hundreds of millions in assets and back accounts.

Another problem occurred occasionally. Some people would try to reach into her pockets. When they did, they would disappear, never to be seen again. She had a special way of dealing with crooked politicians and cops. Benny and Joe and Candy would drug them. They were conscious but unable to move. She and the men would shatter their knees, pulverize the bones in both of their hands, burn out their eyes, cut out their tongues, and poke out their ear drums. All the while telling them what she was going to do before Benny and Joe did it. Benny and Joe would nail a sign to their chest that read, "I am a crooked public servant." Over the years, a Chicago mayor, a police commissioner, two police chiefs, some dirty cops and five or six Chicago city alderman got the treatment. Benny and Joe would dump them on the steps of city hall. After a while, people got the message. Don't reach into Candy's pockets.

On Candy's last trip to the islands, Toney and her decided she was going to retire. She had to return to Chicago on last time to pass the business to Benny and Joe and Ann. The night before she left for Chicago, she and Toney sat on the veranda of Toney's plush beach house talking about getting married.

On the way home from the airport, Candy told Ann that she was returning to the islands and getting married. She told Ann she was passing the business to her, Benny, and Joe. A third each. It meant the three would be splitting close to three to four million a month after expenses.

"Are you at least going to be here for your birthday?" asked Ann.

"Maybe," Candy replied. "Take me to the bar so the men, you, and I can transfer the business today."

"You're really leaving, aren't you?" Ann answered sort of crying.

"Yes, I am," Candy answered.

"I'll miss you. I love you. I wish you wouldn't go," Ann said with tears in her eyes.

At the bar, Candy, the two men, and Ann sat in the office discussing the men and Ann taking over the business effective that day. After the men left the office, Ann lost it. She started to cry.

"Please don't leave me. I love you. How can you marry a man after I loved you. Haven't I been devoted and good to you. Satisfied your every need?"

"Ann, I'll always love you. There is a place in my heart that I save just for you, but as life goes on, I'm sure you'll find another to love. Besides, we can keep in touch and visit from time to time. Pull yourself together. You don't want the men to see you carrying on so, do you?" stated Candy sternly. "You and the men need to get together and work things out with the business. I have things I have to do."

Ann left the office. Candy had a bad feeling concerning Ann's reaction to her news. It quickly passed. She was in love and getting married. For now, that's all she cared about.

That night, Ann lavished Candy with love and affection. No one had ever pleasured her more. "Today is your birthday, Candy. The men and I have a special party for you today," Ann said.

"That's good," Candy replied. "That way I can say good bye to everybody at once. As Candy packed up her things for her move to the islands, an ill feeling came over her. She wasn't sure how far Ann would go to keep her from leaving. Candy put a gun in her bag. As much as she loved Ann, Ann was very unpredictable and maybe a threat.

That evening, Candy went to the bar. Joe and Ann were already there. She didn't see Benny and his brother. This bothered her some. All the women had already placed her birthday cards in the basket.

"Where is Benny and his brother?" Candy asked.

"We need to talk to you about that. Can we talk in your office?" asked Joe.

"Sure thing," replied Candy knowing her ill feeling was coming true.

They went into the office. Candy sat at her desk. "Ann, will you please get us all a drink?"

"Okay," Ann said.

"Don't bother," Joe stated. "She won't have time to drink it anyway."

Candy looked up from her desk. Joe was pointing a gun at her.

"I don't understand, Joe," Candy said. "I've given you three the business on a silver platter. What more do you want?.

"This isn't about the business," Joe answered.

"What is it about," Candy asked.

"You bitch, you killed my brother. Worse yet, you did it in a way that shamed him," he said angrily.

"How do you know I killed him," she asked.

"My brother told me what he did to you and how you told him how much you liked it and don't tell nobody you and he were going out that night. If you would have come to me, I would have done what needed doing, but I would not have shamed him in the process, you bitch."

"Let me guess. Benny and his brother don't work for the company no more," she stated.

"Good guess," said Ann.

"What did I do to you, Ann?" she asked.

"I'm supposed to be here while you're someplace else, giving yourself to some man. You cold hearted bitch. I loved you, and this is how you treat me," Ann said crying.

"Can I have a last cigarette," Candy asked.

"Sure," answered Joe.

"Damn it, Joe. Do it and be done with it," Ann demanded.

Joe looked at Ann. At that moment Candy took a gun from her bag and shot Joe dead. Meanwhile, Ann had a gun and shot Candy twice. Before going down, Candy shot Ann twice. Candy and Joe lay dead. Although seriously wounded, Ann was not dead.

A few days later, Ann woke up in the hospital hand cuffed to the bed. There was a uniform cop sitting in a chair in the room.

"What's going on," Ann demanded to know.

"You're alive. It was all touch and go for a while," said the cop.

"Why am I hand cuffed to the bed?" Ann demanded to know.

"As soon as you're healthy enough, you'll be tried for murder and drug transferring," said the cop. "Here, read about yourself in the paper," he said as he handed the paper to her.

The D.A. was asking for the death sentence. The trial and sentencing hearing went so fast, it was a blur. She was sent to death row. While on death row, she wrote her account of her and Candy's life and the business. Toney had Candy's body flown to the islands where he gave her a sendoff as good as any head of state. He put an eight foot high statue of Aphrodite's, the goddess of love at her grave. Toney inherited the estate worth a hundred and fifty million dollars from Candy.

"They asked me what I wanted for my last meal. I told them I wanted a large member full of nature's juices. Damn if they didn't grant me my last request. But I digress. I love you, Candy. I always will. I hope you can forgive me for what I did to you. Candy, you were right. Get greedy, get dead. See you on the other side."

When they came to take her to the chair, Ann handed a large envelope to the chaplain. "Please, Chaplain, Will you mail this for me."

"Of course," he replied.

As Dan Walters, syndicated writer, finished reading Ann's account, he sipped his drink and puffed on his cigar and said out loud, "Hell of a story."

The End

Be a character in the story.
LIST OF STORY CHARACTERS

The drunk passenger

The trip you will never forget.

GATE 13

I left my hotel at 4:30 AM this morning. I had until 5:45 AM to get through security and check in my bags and get to the departure gate. I made it with twenty minutes to spare. I still had not had my morning coffee. I need it bad! My ass was draggin'. Little sleep, no breakfast and a hangover that would kill most. I made it to the gate anyway. Near the gate was a donut shop! Things were looking up. $12 was a lot for a large coffee and two bear claws but I didn't really care. My needs were great. The bear claws went fast, the coffee no so much. I savored it like fine wine. It hit the spot. An announcement came over the PA "Flight 666 for Las Vegas now loading at Gate 13".

I was among the last to board. It was a full flight. Seated in a row with a middle aged man and woman, I stood out older than both of them and not dressed near as nice. Not caring, I buckled in , closed my eyes and went to sleep. Knowing I'd be in Vegas in 3 hours give or take a few minutes.

I was awakened by a loud noise and a jolt to my seat.

There was speaking "Put your oxygen masks on, if with small children, put your mask on first then the child's mask. Keep seat belts on snug. We're going to make a crash landing."

Looking out the window, there were flames coming from the engines. We were losing altitude fast!

The man sitting next to me seemed to be unconscious. I put his mask on him. The woman was hysterical, others were as well. Some prayed. Looking out the window, I saw planted fields, woods and a river coming close fast.

Speaking "Put your heads between your legs in a bent over postion. Brace for a water landing."

I saw the color had left in the man seated next to me. I think he was dead. I didn't have time to worry about it. the plane hit hard. I thought "time to pray" and I did. Many screamed.

The woman in my row stopped screaming.

 I said to myself, I think I'm alive. I still could hear people carrying on. Thank you God!

I tried to sit up in my seat. I hit something hard shoulder high. I unfastened my seat belt and got out of my seat.

A tree branch had penetrated the plane. The woman sitting next to me in my row was impaled by the branch. Her body twitching, tears streamed down her face. She was alive for how long I don't know. She didn't make a sound. She looked at me and said "Help me."

I felt helpless.

This lasted for a short time.

Can you hear me? I asked her.

I'm going to die she said.

Let's hope not I replied.

It hurts, pull it out she begged.

If I do, you'll bleed to death. I told her. Can you feel or move your arms or legs I asked realizing she had died.

I closed her eyes. The passengers were beginning to calm down and get it together.

A crew member had opened the cabin door of the plane to allow passengers to exit the plane.

We had landed on the water and skipped to shore on the far side of the river.

As I looked around, most of the passengers had left their seats and were exiting the plane.

The plane crew kept repeating, "Stay close to the plane so we don't lose anyone and can get a head count."

Blood spewed from the woman's mouth. The branch must have penetrated her lungs. I was saddened by her death. I didn't know her name or why.

A crew member asked me if I was ok.

I stood up and said "They're both dead. I think he had a heart attack and she was impaled by a tree branch. And I need a stiff drink!"

As I walked toward the exit, I heard loud chatter from outside the plane.

Somebody screamed, "I've been bit by a snake!"

Others did the same.

It started an instant panic.

"Everybody back on the plane NOW!" ordered the crew.

The plane came to rest on a rattle snake nest. Over half the passengers were bit and most of them more than once. Some still lay on the ground dead or dying while snakes crawled over their bodies. Of those bitten that made it back to the plane, were becoming comatose and dying. Only 60 passengers didn't get bitten.

They were getting ugly, demanding answers from the crew that survived the snakes.
 I suggested serving some food and liquor to the passengers still uneasy, hearing the rattle snakes outside the plane.

The passengers calmed down somewhat after having a few drinks.

I felt someone touch me on my shoulder.

A pleasant voice woke me.

"Sir, Sir, we've landed in Las Vegas, you must have been tired. You slept the entire flight."

THE END

SPARE ME

Be a character in the story.

LIST OF STORY CHARACTERS

The woman

Terry

She was a beautiful and
mysterious woman

SPARE ME

Her hair was silver and white. She was an attractive older woman. She had blue eyes and red lipstick, slender and well endowed. She moved with grace and lots of confidence and proud. Her smile lit up the room. Being under five feet she still looked every bit a mature woman. She wore a red velvet blouse and jeans that accented her female wiles. Her face lied about her age. She might be sixty but looked much younger. She gave off a warm, and friendly ora. As I sat looking at this woman, I asked myself, is this woman as she looks or is she flying false colors? I had to find out. I couldn't get her out of my mind. She took over my head. She looked too good to be real.

Something wasn't right. I don't know if I admired this woman or feared her. It didn't matter what I did, it was like knowing better and yet venturing where I shouldn't. What was it about this woman?

Her alabaster skin and red lips caused me to want to know her more and more. Not knowing why troubled me deeply. When she left her chair, walking in front of me, I was like a young teen boy looking at his first crush. I wanted to speak to her but couldn't get the words to come out of my mouth. What was it about the woman that made me so befuddled? This had never happened to me before, not even as a young man.

She spoke to me and at first I couldn't focus on her words. Then I felt her hand touch my hand.

"You ok?" She asked.

I found myself apologizing for my unintended rudeness. I looked down at her hand touching my hand and I felt complete fear. Her hand was bare bone, no skin what so ever. I tried to pull my hand away, but couldn't. a comforting voice said, "Don't be afraid, I mean you no harm."

My fear subsided

"Does your hand hurt?" I asked the woman.

"I feel no pain." Stated she. "And as you walk with me you will feel pain no more."

"How so?" I asked the woman.

"you will feel no pain or fear , sadness, or loneliness again."

Once again fear rushed over me. "I have no wish to be numb," I said more afraid.

"You will be deep asleep." She said.

"Who are you?" I asked my voice shaking.

"I am the inner peace you seek," She said, impatient.

"I won't walk with you. Please go away, spare me please spare me." I begged.

"It's not up to me." She said to me.

At that moment, I felt my stomach come into my mouth. There were bright lights and blurred shapes of people in medical garb. I heard a man say, "He's coming around."

The woman was gone. I was glad she was gone and that she had spared me.

I did go to sleep.

When next I opened my eyes I saw an old and dear friend, Terry. We hugged each other for a long time. Finally I spoke. "I heard you had a heart attack."

"Yea I did." Said he. "So you decided to walk with the woman?"

"Yea I guess so." Said I.

She didn't spare me after all.

It's a secret

Be a character in the story.

LIST OF STORY CHARACTERS

Mark - the father

The son's

Marie - the wife

Hannah(scamp)- daughter

Alicia - daughter

The secret would destroy
them.

IT'S A SECRET

Mark and his family are upper middle class. Mark works for the government in a security sensitive job, with political aspirations. His four children are from his first marriage. Their mother died five years ago. Their ages range from 15 to 19 years old. Now mark's second wife differs from his first wife in a number of ways. The biggest difference is Mark's wife's dirty secret.

After four years of marriage, not even the children know their secret. Maria, Mark's wife, is fifteen years younger than Mark and very attractive. She dresses very alluring and is well endowed.

As a family, they get along as well as any family with four teenagers in it. Mark's oldest daughter isn't sure she likes men or women. His two sons are very close to their step mother but not as close as their older sister. Their younger sister doesn't miss anything happening in or outside the family home. Now Hanna is very industrious and has some larceny in her.

Now, Mark and Maria took every avenue to hide their dirty secret. If it got out, it could trash his whole life and career. Only Maria and Mark and her lovers knew the family secret. To make matters worse, Maria thought she might be pregnant. Normally this wouldn't have been a problem. Her and Mark were saying it was theirs. The family was not aware of it. as it turned out, none of Maria's three lovers knew about the others. Maria was sure only two of her three lovers could be the father, but wasn't sure which one of the two

The day came when both of Mark's sons went to see a doctor. They both had developed a rash on … well let's just call it a real sensitive place. Man did it itch! Now because they scratched it, what else? It spread. As it turns out, Mark and Maria also had the rash as well as the older daughter.

When Mark asked his daughter Hanna if she was doing ok, did she have a need to see a doctor? Hanna broke out into a loud, boisterous laughter. It was long and kind of sinister. Mark demanded to know what was so funny. He was very angry. "I'm guessing the chickens have come home to roost." Said Hanna, still laughing. "What's with you? Are you crazy? Are you on drugs or what?" asked Mark very angrily.

Hanna was still laughing and Mark reached out and grabbed Hanna by the throat and slammed her against the wall. His hand against her throat, she was unable to breathe. Desperately, she tried to fight off Mark and she gasped for air. She punched, kicked, and scratched until she succumbed to unconsciousness from lack of air and went limp. After which, Mark bounced her head off the wall until drawing blood from the back of her head. Mark threw her limp body to the floor thinking she was dead.

Mark stood over Hanna's body telling himself "a bad situation just got worse."
Speaking out loud, "Lord I just stepped on my own dick."
Hanna showed no signs of life. Mark was sure she was dead. He picked up Hanna's body threw it over his shoulder, carried it to the basement and stacked it into a storage closed temporarily until he figured out how to get rid of it.

After storing Hanna's body Mark met his two sons coming home from the doctor. Both were angry and worried. They told Mark both of them had been with Maria and their older sister as well as Mark on occasion. Mark asked them if they or Maria had been with Hanna. "Not to our knowledge," they replied.
"What did the doctor say," inquired Mark.
"The doctor said until the test results come back, they couldn't be sure. He gave us this cream to help with the itching until then."
"I haven't seen Maria today. Do you know where she is?" Mark asked. "She said she was going for a drive but didn't say where." answered Mark's oldest son.
"she was upset and crying. She gave me a big hug and told me, "remember, I loved being with you kids. I kind of wish I had been with your father now. I love you." And she drove away.
Mark knew at that point Maria had plans to kill herself.
"Do you know where your sister is?" asked Mark of his sons.
"You mean Hanna?"
No.
"I think Alicia is still sleeping."
Now Alicia is the older sister. The men went to Alicia's room entering Alicia's room they saw her hanging from the chandelier. Around her neck was a note saying. "God forgive me, forgive us all."
Mark, biting his hand was both sad and without any hope for the future. He knew his professional and political career was over. Mark was so deep in numbness and depression he didn't notice his youngest son on his knees throwing up next to him and on him. The wet vomit brought him out of his numbness. He saw his oldest son trying to cut down Alicia from the chandelier while crying tears dripping off his face.
"Now I have two bodies to get rid of," stated Mark aggravated. With that, Mark left the room as Alicia's body was being lowered to the floor. Both brothers asked, "Why? Where did dad go?"
After the brothers covered up their sister with reverence, they went to find dad and were wondering why Alicia's body had to be disposed of. As they neared their dad and Maria's bedroom they heard loud cursing by their father. Looking into the room they witnessed the only time their dad got real emotional.

"Are you alright dad?" asked the boys.

"Why would I not be?" replied Mark. "Now go to the basement and get Hanna and take her to the van and be quick about it." ordered Mark.

They boys replied, "What if she won't come with us, you know how she can be."

"Trust me she'll be real congenial about it," Mark barked, "Now get going!"

"Yes dad." answered the boys.

Mark got Alicia from her room and took her to the van. The boys hadn't brought Hanna from the basement yet. Mark went to the basement to see where the boys went. When Mark reached the basement he found both boys lying face down on the floor dead.

Mark looked in the closet where he put Hanna's body. It was gone. Suddenly, Mark heard loud, sinister laughter over the intercom. A chill came over Mark. His itchy rash was no longer his biggest problem and survival became number one.

Mark knew he had to get out of the house and fast if he was to survive. He heard loud, boisterous, sinister laughter.

"Hey daddy, would you be interested in knowing your rash is a flesh eating disease? If not it will eventually cover your entire body. Maria and Alicia both knew, that's why they killed themselves. I killed my brothers. I loved them and didn't want them to suffer. Eventually the pain is unbearable, it causes madness. There is no cure. Enjoy daddy!" stated Hanna, ending with loud, boisterous, continual sinister laughter.

Mark fell on his knees and screamed "NOOOOOOOOOOO"

THE END

Is Everything Free in America?

Be a character in the story.
LIST OF STORY CHARACTERS

Juan   husband
Juanita   wife
Lawyer
Tony   fixer

Is it really free.....

IS EVERYTHING IN AMERICA FREE?

Juan came to America as an illegal from Mexico at 15 years old. Most of his family was still in Mexico. Our government is allowing illegals to stay in America and receive Medicaid, food stamps, free legal services and free housing. By executive order by the President any household willing to host an illegal child in America will receive $6,100.00per month tax freee and food stamps, free education for the quest child. Now that you have a basic background of the actual facts, let's begin my story.

Juan an wanita live in Chicago. They came to America illegally 8 years ago. Juan in a carpenter and a union member and his wife, Wanita cleans houses for a living. Neither speak English very well. They saw the ad about the host family program and it's benefits on a Spanish TV channel. Juan and wanita applied for and got accepted by the quest host program. Soon after they got into the program they needed to bring on more help. Tow of their cousins came on board. By now they had leased several apartment buildings and warehouses for food distributions. They also hired host parents at $1,000.00 a month and expenses. By the end of the first year, the family was splitting $600,000.00 a month after expenses, tax free. Plus $50,000.00 a month in cash from food stamp sales. They got so big they had to hire two house parent managers at $10,000.00 a month to supervise all the host families. As well as more warehouse workers and managers. They had a $5,000.00 a month budget to pay them. Now all those buildings wre in gang infested areas. The quest children got involved with drug dealing, prostitution and extortion. When they got caught, the government paid their legal bills. The family realized the large amounts of cash had to be put in off shore accounts.
Now not knowing who would win the upcoming election they family thought the program might be discontinued. Because of this fact, they moved millions to foreign banks.
Come a warm sunny day, two men paid a visit to Juan and Wanita. Both well dressed and rather large. They introduced themselves as Agent Miller from the federal Fraud Department and Attorney Myers of the INS. They started by telling Juan and Wanita their cousins had signed over all their bank accounts and family

shares over to them and from this day on, Juan and Wanita had two new partners, Miller and Myers. Juan and Wanita will pay $300,000.00to Miller and Myers each month on the second of each month and $50,000.00for each day it's late. As well as $1.4 million of previous years profits.

"Now we're not greedy we only want half of the $1.4 million plus $300,000.00 from your share each month. Now you do have the option of not complying with our request, however, if you don't you will be arrested and tried for food stamp fraud, running a prostitution ring, drug trafficking and being in America illegally. You will be sent to prison where you will maybe be killed by our associates. Should you comply with our request you will bring $300,000.00 a month in cash to attorney Ducon's office by 11 AM tomorrow. If you don't, there is a $50,000.00 a day late charge. After three days you will be turned over to our collection department. Things could get unpleasant. Do you have any questions?

Juan and Wanita said nothing.

"Your silence tells me you understand," stated Mr. Miller. "See you tomorrow." The two men left.

Their day went down hill. Juan & Wanita talked for a time. Both looked out the window. A man and woman sat in a parked care across the street. It was a big black car with tinted windows. "Juan, do you think the people in the car work for Mr. Miller?" asked Wanita.

"I don't know." He replied. "I'll talk to tony and see if he can help us."

"Tony said for $150,000.00 he'll make our problem go away." Juan said later.

The next day the car was still there. Two days later the car was still there. Wanita and Juan got the $300,000.00 cash and the $150,000.00 late charge and went to the lawyer's office. After waiting an hour, the secretary told them they could go in. There were two chairs empty, Tony sat in the third. Attorney Ducan greeted them with a smile.

"Welcome Juan and Wanita, better late than never. I believe you know Tony, he tells me you agreed to pay him to be your go between. I approve, so each and every month you will pay him $150,000.00 from your share. Seeing as you brought him into the deal. Any communication concerning our business will go through him. He is your boss from now on. Should I be bothered in the future will cost you more and might be unpleasant for you. Do you understand? Do you have all the money?" He went on.

Juan said "Yes sir."

"Give it to Tony. We won't meet again." The lawyer said, no longer smiling. "You folks have a real nice day." And he left the room.

Tony told Juan and Wanita all they would be are managers of the business and would get a generous and total of $50,000.00 and the right to live.

"Any questions?"

"No" replied Juan.

"Remember your new payment is $450.000.00. Don't be late! Don't forget my clients half of the 1.4 million each month. We're done here. Oh, before I forget, from time to time, packages will be delivered to the house homes. You will pick them up there and bring them to me unopened. If opened, you will call me from that location at that time, since no one should work fro free, you get an extra $10,000.00 a month for this service. Understand?"

"Yes sir" replied both Juan and Wanita.

Now maybe this story is fiction, maybe not.

Maybe everything in America isn't free.

Or is it?

I am a Doctor

Be a character in the story.

LIST OF STORY CHARACTERS

Dr. Barnes

Dr. Matters

Mamy Lou – Joseph's lover

Daniel – Dr. Barnes lover

Joseph – Slave master

Young black woman goes to England and becomes a doctor and comes to America in 1850.

I am a Doctor

As the ship drew near the docks of Charleston Harbor Dr. Barnes stood on the deck of the ship looking at the many ships already there. It was a beautiful sunny day she was both young and beautiful she was proud that she graduated at the top of her class at Cambridge. After all for a woman to get a medical degree in the year 1855 was unheard of, especially for a black woman. Her mother was a slave that escaped to the north before she was born. Her father was born up north. Both her parents told her it is illegal for blacks to read or write. Dr. Barnes being freeborn felt she had nothing to worry about.

As she walked down the gang way carrying her medical bag, she saw number of black men and women chained together being led down the dock by two large white men carrying whips.

One of the white men commented to the other, "look at the black woman dressed like a white woman."

The other man replied,   "She would bring a good price."

Dr. Barnes started getting an uneasy feeling, she quickened her step. When she saw the man and women in the slave lines she was sadden and frightened. Every white she passed gave her a dirty look. She was relieved after she passed by the slave auction platform and got to the Main Street. The doctor found what she was looking for. The sign said "Dr. Matters-Physician and Embalming Services."

When Dr. Barnes entered Dr. Matters waiting room there were men and women dressed in fine clothing. The doctor's receptionist told her Dr. Matters did not treat blacks.

"I'm not a patient my name is Dr. Barnes I am here to see the Dr. on business."

"You can't be a doctor it's against the law to teach blacks to read and write," said the receptionist with an angry voice.

"I'm from England," said the Dr.

I'm going to call the constable if you don't leave immediately, the receptionist declared. This waiting room is for whites only.

Where is the waiting room for blacks? asked the doctor.

There is none replied the receptionist.

She went through a door off the waiting room. The white patients began to whisper amongst themselves. Moments later two constables entered the waiting room.

We need to see your pass, order the constables.

I don't have one the Dr. replied why do I need a pass?

The constables dragged the Dr. away protesting loudly. The doctor spent the rest of the day and all that night in a 6 x 6 cell with no bad and no place to sit. There was a bucket in the corner to relieve herself. The few times she protested a man came and threw a bucket of water on her and told her to be quiet or he would beat her. She slept sitting in a corner that night. Her fine grass was wet and dirty. They took her medical bag away as well as medical certificate. She was without food and water since she was arrested. She was awakened that morning when a heavy white man with a thick mustache throwing water on her. Standing next to that man was a tall man holding some shackles.

The constable stated she claims to be a doctor. When we brought her here she had a medical bag and doctor certificate. I want my reward before you can take her away the constable demanded.

The man with the shackles gave him some cash and said "open the door."

Again the Dr. protested. It took both men to put the shackles on her. The man put her in a wagon with bars on it. She protested the whole time.

Finally the man told her if she didn't be quiet he would use a whip on her. He said he didn't want to because he didn't want to lose money by disfiguring her.

It didn't take long for the wagon to reach the slave auction platform and holding pens.

I am a doctor she declared once again not a slave.

The man did not reply.

The man stopped the wagon and walked to the back of the wagon.

Now I suggest you listen real good. It's against the law for slaves to know how to read and write. In fact you could be hung for violating the law as well as the person who taught you how to read and write. Do you understand, the man asked the doctor. I suggest you listen real good.

I'm not a slave I'm a doctor the Dr. declared with anger.

Can you prove you're not a slave the man asked.

I saw the constable hand you my medical bag and medical certificate said the Dr.

I'll tell you what after I get you prepared and secure so you can't run off I'll check it out said the man.

You two come here speaking to the slave handlers. Get her cleaned up and if you sample the merchandise don't bruise or mar her body.

The Dr. became concerned she knew what was next. She fought with all her strength to not go with the two men to no avail. She heard the slave master yell "don't bruise her"

The dr. remembered her mother telling her how common it was for whites to rape young black women and children with no consequences. The two men took the dr. into a building with a wood floor and began ripping off her clothes. When the dr. realized protesting and fighting the two men wasn't doing any good, she went limp closed her eyes and lay naked on the floor. She could feel the two men using her and talking to each other. When they were done, they tried to get her up. The dr. didn't respond. She didn't move at all.

One man said to the other, I think we are in trouble.

The other man said, throw water on her, see if that brings her around.

As the dr. lay on the floor listening to the men but not moving, she knew they would pay for their actions.

Let's put a gown on her and get the boss. Let's not tell him we used her.

The dr. heard them leave and shut the door behind them. The men had removed her shackles to use her. She got up off the floor and looked out the door. There was nobody around. The doctor left the building and headed for parts unknown. She didn't run, she didn't want to look suspicious. She did however move with a quick step never looking any white people in the face.

The two men and the slave master went into the building where they left the dr. On the floor laid the shackles she had on. The slave master ordered one of the men to fetch the constable. When the constable arrived, the slave master told the constable he wanted the two men that let the doctor escape arrested and held for ??? court. When they were in court the slave master asked for $5,000 a piece for losing the dr. The judge ordered both men to pay the money.

They said they didn't have it. The men were ordered sold in the servitude and sold for their debt. The dr. was hungry and thirsty since she hadn't eaten in days. She was ready to collapse from exhaustion. She could go no further. She stopped and sat down by a wagon. A large older black man touched her on her arm.

Girl you don't look so good

Help me please the dr. exclaimed.

I'll do anything I can said the man.

Do you have any food and water the dr. asked.

The man got some fruit out of the back of the wagon and gave her water.

You a runaway the man asked?

No she replied, I'm a dr. from England. The constable and slave master don't believe me.

Get on the wagon, the man told her as he handed her some more fruit and water. Best we get you away from here.

As the man drove the wagon he asked, " If you aint a runaway where's your doctor paper?"

The constable took them, gave them to the lave master, I didn't think it smart to ask him for them when I left. They raped me repeatedly. They were going to sell me. I am not a slave. They didn't feed me or give me any water. They told me I could be put to death for knowing how to read and write.

He told you right, the man said, best you don't let on you read and write.

Where are we going? She asked.

My master has a plantation about three hours from here.

Let me off then.

Best you stay with me. They catch you alone, they rape you and maybe hang afterward. Master has a lot of slaves. You don't draw no attention to yourself, nobody notice, don't tell nobody you a doctor. You should blend in.

On the ride to the plantation, the man said his name was James. The master was called Master Joseph, kind and generous. His wife liked using the women slaves and enjoyed being abusive to them if they didn't please her. One time she had one hung because she refused to please her. She was 16 year old. You best keep low, the master is drunk most of the time. That will make it easier for you to go unnoticed. When we get there, I'll take you to Mamy Lou. She see you get food and such. You'll work in the cook house, away from the master's wife for she'll want you sure, she see you.

As the wagon went up the long drive to the mansion, she saw many slaves, both black and white

Are the whites slaves too? The doctor asked.

Yes replied James, there are as many white slaves as there are blacks on the plantation. Master Joseph black you know.

You say a slave can own slaves? Asked the doctor.

No replied James, he free born like myself? Said the doctor, why do they believe him and not me?

He has papers and you don't replied James. Let's see how it goes maybe Mamy Lou talk to the master for you. Until then you be invisible OK?

Mamy Lou came out to meet the wagon. She is 30 years old and very attractive with a big smile.

Good day Papa, she said

Good day replied James, Doctor, this is Mamy Lou, my daughter, she has the master's ear. If anybody can help you it's her.

We won't use that tern doctor for the time being. For your own safety. By and by I'll speak to the master on your behalf. Stated Mamy Lou. Come inside and tell me all about it, while you talk, I'll make some food for you.

The two women walked into the building and James unloaded the wagon. The two women talked for some time. After hearing the doctor's story Mamy Lou told her, "We will call you Jodie, we do this to keep your identity secret for your safety until I can speak to the master about you. I be with him three or four times a week. That's the best time to ask him for things he is a kind and generous man and passionate. Meanwhile, you stay and work with me. Tell no one your real name or that you are a doctor.

Days become weeks and months, they day came when she realized she was with child. When she told Mamy Lou, Mamy Lou told Jodie any babies born on the plantation were the master's property. She went on, being free born that may not be the case, which buck were you with?

A buck didn't do it, the slave handlers at the port auction pens raped me before I escaped. Jodie said.

We can wait no longer, I be with the master today. He's been kinda surley these days that's why I been putting it off. I haven't been with him for almost two weeks now, his wife been sick. Stated Mamy Lou.

Mamy, I am a doctor, it's as good a time as any to let the master know that. Declared Jodie

I don't know sure the master wont' turn you into the law for knowing how to read and write. If your willing to take a chance come with me.

The two women went to see the master. The master was with his wife. She was very sick.

What do you want Mamy Lou? asked the master.

Master, this woman is a doctor, maybe she can comfort your wife.

How is she a doctor? Asked the master.

Is that really important? Asked Mamy Lou.

Come closer girl, ordered the master, are you really a doctor?

Yes sir replied Jodie, I got my degree from Cambridge University in England.

Step up and help my wife, please? Asked the master.

The doctor examined the patient. She pulled the blankets off the patient and told Mamy Lou.

"Get me a lot of towels and fill both tubs with cool water.

Mamy Lou did.

Sir this woman has the fever. If we don't cool her down she will die.

The master ordered all the slaves to fetch water quickly. He ordered others to cary his wife to the tub and put her in the tub.

Sir it would be more effective if she were undressed so the water can have direct contact with her body. Said the doctor.

After a day or two passed the patient's fever broke and she lay in bed awake taking food and water.

She asked her husband what was going on.

He told her Dr. Barnes saved her life and that she had the fever.

Who's Dr. Barnes? She asked.

Dr. Barnes is a you black woman who went to medical school in England. You rest now. Try to get some sleep. Mamy Lou, fetch the doctor and bring her to my study.

I ask your pardon master, the doctor is tending some of the blacks that took sick.

Take me to where she is now and be quick about it! he demanded.

When they reached the river, they saw some blacks sitting in the water, other blacks were keeping the sick from falling under the water and drowning.

What's going on here, where's the overseer? asked the master in a loud demanding voice.

He's dead the doctor answered. He refused to let me treat him. Most of the sick are getting better, some didn't make it. I've isolated the sick so more don't get sick. Three hundred of the sick will probably live. Forty five of the sick have died including the overseer. I've found no new cases, I think we've got it under control. The master sat down on a fallen tree, scratched his head. He was speechless.

Moments later he asked, are you pregnant doctor?

Yes, six months pregnant and real tired, she answered.

Come sit here with me, he ordered.

She did.

"Mamy Lou go to the main house and prepare a bedroom for the doctor. See she has a pitcher of water, wash basin, an excuse me and fresh fruit in the room. Go do it now!

Yes master, she replied.

Doctor form this day on, you live in the main house, you will be responsible for the care of my family and all others on the plantation. Anything you want or need to do that or to deal with your pregnancy let me know.

Thank you replied the doctor, all I want now is sleep, I've been awake for so long I've lost count of how many days it has been.

The master ordered one of the male slaves to fetch a wagon to carry the doctor to the main house. At the house the mster took the doctor to her room. Mamy Lou was finishing making the bed. Mamy Lou, you will tend to every need the doctor might have any time of the day or night. Do you understand?

Yes, master.

I'd like to take a bath before I do to bed, stated the doctor.

See to it, ordered the master to Mamy Lou

Yes master, replied Mamy lou.

As Mamy Lou bathed the doctor she told her, "today I went from head slave and mistress to the master, to being your personal slave."

Mamy Lou, as far as I'm concerned, you still the master 's mistress. As far as being my slave, let's say your my professional assistatnt and good friend. If you want I'll teach you some medical things.

That be wonderful said Mamy Lou, with joy in her voice.

After bathing the doctor went to bed. She slept all that night and most of the next day. She was awakened by Mamy Lou. She was all charged up.

Doctor the master wants you to join him and some dinner guests at four today. You got to hurry it's already 2:3o, you been sleeping a long time. The master bought you these beautiful clothes to wear. I'll help you get dressed and fix your hair.

Good morning Mamy Lou. Bring me some coffee, give me a moment to wake up and then repeat everything you said, the doctor said yawning.

Yes, doctor, Mamy Lou answered as she poured coffee for the doctor.

Now start over and tell me everything the master said.

After getting dressed, the doctor looked a beautiful young woman of means. When the doctor entered the large lavish dining room with all the trappings of a wealthy land owner of the day, sitting at a long dining table was the master, his wife and four others new to her.

All the men sitting at the table stood, including the master.

Mamy Lou standing behind the Dr. said, I never thought Id'd see the day white folks stand up when a black woman entered a room. The Dr. turned to Mamy Lou and said, hush go about your business.

Yes Doctor, replied Mamy lou as she turned and walked away talking to herself under her breath. Doctor please come in permit me to introduce you to my guest. As the master walked her to the table of the guests and introduced each one to her. All of means. The one guest that stood out the most was Doctor Matters and his receptionist wife. Doctor Barnes continued to smile and be gracious anyway. Her medical bag was on the table. Sitting at the table was chief constable. The master introduced her to his son, Daniel, like his mother he was white. The master pulled a chair from the table an invited her to sit next to his son. Daniel was tall, well built and a handsome man twenty five years old. Doctor I'm told my mother owes her life to you. I am most grateful, thank you!

Before the doctor could respond, Dr. Matters said, after learning about your success treating the collera outbreak, I'm truly impressed. I heard about your exploits when you came to my office to see me. It should not have happened. I'd be proud if you would join my medical practice. Before doctor Barnes could answer, Joseph spoke, "Let's get dinner started." He ordered the servants to pour everyone some wine and bring on the food. Doctor Barnes was glad, besides being overwhelmed, she was real hungry. She needed time to think about everything said at the table. The meal was delicious. The conversation during dinner was friendly, light and pleasant. With the exception of doctor Matters wife, everybody seemed to enjoy the meal.

After the meal, Joseph gave doctor Barnes her medical bag and medical certificate and told her she had definitely earned them. He asked her, Doctor Matters and Daniel to join him in the study. Joseph ordered a servant to bring brandy to his study. Joseph and Doctor Matters discussed Doctor Barnes joining Doctor Matters practice. Finally Joseph asked Doctor Barnes how she felt about joining Doctor Matters practice.

I don't think your patients would accept being treated by a black doctor answered Doctor Barnes.

Maybe you start out handling embalming and eventually move up to treating the patients replied Doctor Matters.

Like yourself I'm a doctor that's what my certificate says and that's what I'm going to do but thank you for your generous offer Doctor Matters. Replied Doctor Barnes

As the two doctors continued to talk about it. why don't you stay here and be the plantation doctor suggested Daniel.

Your welcome to do that if you choose to do so, stated Joseph.

I'd like that Doctor Barnes answered with a smile on her face.

Then it's agreed, declared Joseph.

Joseph can I talk to you in private? Asked Doctor Matters.

Ok replied Joseph.

Daniel won't you show Doctor Barnes some of the plantation.

Yes sir with pleasure answered Daniel.

Daniel and Doctor Barnes left the study arm in arm. After a short time walking around the plantation still arm in arm becoming even closer. Meanwhile, Doctor Matters was trying to buy Doctor Barnes from Joseph, offering as much as fifteen thousand dollars. While Doctor Barnes and Daniel sat by a babbling brook, they heard gun shots coming from the house. They saw pillars of smoke in the sky and heard loud screams. When they reached the house, they saw the house was engulfed in flames.

    Joseph and the male white dinner guests including Doctor Matters and the chief constable lay on the lawn dead.

    The women were frantic with fear and grief.

Daniel asked his mother what happened, "who did this"

Jay haws his mother replied

I heard of thiem through they are murderous apalitionists trying to stop slavery by killing plantation owners one at a time.

To Doctor Barnes dismay, she realized her medical bag and medical certificate wer in the burning house gone forever.

As Daniel and his mother knelt by Joseph grieving, Doctor Barnes tried to comfort them.

Help him! Daniel demanded of Doctor Barnes.

I wish I could, replied Doctor Barnes but he has passed on. I'm sorry, I really liked Joseph, he was a kind generous man.

Mamy Lou walked to Doctor Barnes, Is he, she began to ask.

Yes, said Doctor Barnes, Get a blanket to cover him.

Doctor Barnes checked the others. They were all dead. Daniel ordered a black to fetch a constable straight away.

Doctor Matters wife blamed Doctor Barnes for her husband's death.

Daniel told her she was wrong and she should grieve without blaming Doctor Barnes. When the constable arrived, Doctor Matters wife again blamed Doctor Barnes for her husband's death.

Daniel told him he and Doctor Barnes were nowhere near the mansion when the shooting took place, that his mother said, Jay Hawks did it.

Is that true? The constable asked Joseph's wife

Yes, she replied, the Jay Hawks dragged the men outside this house, shot them dead and set the house a fire and told the slaves they were all free.

Joseph sold the pregenant slave, called Doctor Barnes to my husband, just before he was murdered, declared Doctor Matters wife.

She lies, stated Daniel, if she is telling the truth, have her show proof here and now.

Do you have a bill of sale? The constable asked Doctor Matters wife.

He had a bill of sale but the Jay Hawks took if off his body after they killed him. She said with an angry frustrated voice.

Constable, Joseph made a gift of Doctor Barnes to my son while we all sat at the table having dinner, said Joseph's wife. Doctor Matters tried to buy her, Joseph told Doctor Matters she wasn't for sale at any price. Constable, Doctor Matters wife has lied no less than three times, might she be in violation of the law? Joseph's wife demanded to know.

Doctor Barnes didn't like hearing she was a gift to the man she had been passionate with.

Is anything you have said here today concerning the events of the day that you might have said in error? Asked the constable of Doctor Matters wife.

All I know is my husband is dead, she blurted out, crying.

Joseph's wife tried to comfort her and immediately got rudely rebuked.

Come with me, said Daniel, to Doctor Barnes

Yes, master answered Doctor Barnes, coldly as she went with Daniel.

As the tow walked away from the crowd, Daniel asked why the doctor was getting so cold.

She replied, you should know. Chattel call their owner's master.

My mother did that to end your status conversation with the constable for your benefit. You should be grateful. Replied Daniel. I don' t want you to be chattel, I want you to be my wife, I love you.

Doctor Barnes stopped walking and sat down on a nearby bench. Daniel stopped walking and sat down next to her.

Why do you want ot marry me, I am with child by another man by rape. It would bring shame to your family, said Doctor Barnes. With tears in her eyes she continued, When I marry it will be as a free woman and doctor. You would have to accept, love and care for my baby as your own.

Daniel moved closer to Doctor Barnes and put his arm around her and pulled her closer to him. Holding her tight he said, I won't have it any other way. I love you. Your child will be my child and heir. We will love and raise it together.

How will your mother accept us getting married? She asked.

I believe how we feel about it is what is important. He replied, don't you?

I love you as well, marrying you would make me very happy. However, being with child we should have a small private wedding and have a reception after the baby is born. Would you agree? Replied Doctor Barnes.

Yes answered Daniel.

As the two sat and talked and held each other close Daniel's mother and the constable approached them. Doctor Barnes began getting real uneasy.

This cannot be good news. She told Daniel as she held his hand tight.

I won't let any harm come to you, Daniel answered her.

Daniel, I have to take this slave into custody, she has broken the law by knowing how to read and write. Said the constable.

This slave is mine therefore it is my right to punish her not yours! He declared in an angry and authoritative voice.

I'll have to talk to the magistrate and get back to you. Meantime she can stay here for now. Said the constable.

After the constable was out of eyeshot Daniel told his mother that Doctor Barnes and him were engaged to be married and he was giving her free papers.

I love her, we want to be married as soon as possible.

Son, I'm both sad and happy for you but she has broken the law, how do we deal with that? His mother asked.

I will give her free papers and date them for the date she arrived here. Daniel stated.

What if Doctor Matters wife challenges that? asked his mother. His wife is bitter. According to the law Doctor Barnes could be hung without a trial if you truly love this woman and want to marry her I suggest you and her go up north immediately. Give things here a chance to subside. Maybe come back in a year or two.

Your mother is right you know. Stated Doctor Barnes.

I'll have James fetch the surry straight away.

I suggest you tell no one your destination. If anyone asks tell them you and your slave are going to visit kin and the slave is to warm your bed at night.

I don't like being called a slave, stated Doctor Barnes.

Would you rather hand asked Daniel's mother. You two don't have any time to waste. Daniel, I'll pack your velice and food for the road. Doctor Barnes you need to change your clothes as to look more like a slave. Write me when you get settled up north. Now get moving, time is passing. Stated Daniel's mother. May God watch over you both.

Daniel hugged his mother as did Doctor Barnes. The sun having set made Daniel and Doctor Barnes feel at east while traveling north. Daniel was saddened at his father's death and regretted not being able to be at his father's send off.

As the two head north they talked about the future. Doctor Barnes told Daniel all about her family. Her father has a successful blacksmith business, her mother is a school teacher, her younger brother is working hard at becoming a lawyer. Daniel was surprised to hear how blacks had such opportunities up north.

At sunrise the next morning, Daniel woke up Doctor Barnes. He gave her a tender good morning kiss and told her they are going to stop and eat and stretch their legs some. As they ate and rested, Doctor Barnes asked how much further they had to go.

I'm not real sure replied Daniel, at least a day maybe two. The horses need water and rest, me too. I can drive a spell if you want. Stated Doctor Barnes

Wake me in tow hours, Daniel said as he laid down and closed his eyes and went to sleep. Doctor Barnes looked at Daniel lovingly as he slept. She was happy, she knew once they got up north, everything would be good. Doctor Barnes went into a wooded area to relieve herself. While doing so she heard voices one was Daniel's. when she cautiously left the wooded area, she saw four covered cargo wagons that had signs reading "Murphy's Freight Company. Daniel offered the men drivgin the wagons coffee and food. The men seemed harmless when Doctor Barnes reached Daniel's side.

One driver commented to Daniel, it looks like your going to increase your inventory.

Yes replied Daniel

You sell that baby it be pure profit, a driver said.

True enough, Daniel replied, you men have a good trip, we have to move on. As he put his belongings in the surrey and helped Doctor Barnes in the Surry.

How much? Doctor Barnes heard one of the drivers ask.

No charge for the food and coffee have a good trip now. Daniel answered as he took the reins in hand.

I was speaking about the black, how much? The driver asked again.

This made Doctor Barnes uneasy, Daniel took two pistols from under the seat and gave Doctor Barnes one and kept one.

She's not for sale, stated Daniel. But thank you for your interest.

With that they pulled away from the drivers.

Do you expect trouble from them, asked Doctor Barnes..

I hope not stated Daniel, we will keep our guns handy just in case.

After taking turns driving while the other slept, stopping only to let the horses rest and graze in the grass and take water. After two full days travel, Doctor Barnes started experiencing severe pain and was bleeding.

Daniel, I'm losing the baby with the pain and bleeding. I'm sure of it.

Do you want to stop and rest? Daniel asked concerned.

No just get me across the Ohio so me and our baby can be born on free soil, answered Doctor Barnes in pain.

Doctor Barnes lay in Daniel's arms while the horses were driving themselves. It was only a short time when Doctor Barnes let out a loud scream of agony. Daniel began to cry and whale with grief his wife was dead. Daniel held his wife close to his chest. He'd lay her to rest in free soil after crossing the Ohio on a river ferry for wagons. Daniel laid his wife and his unborn child to rest under a big shade tree. He wept some and headed back home. He'd wire Doctor Barnes family when he came to town. It would be a long ride home for Daniel, he had his memories with Doctor Barnes to keep him company.

Lucky Day

Be a character in the story.
LIST OF STORY CHARACTERS

Rob – Lucky winner
Linda – his wife
Lou - Stranger
Josh – son

Lottery winners day of
shopping

A Lucky Day

Rob walked down the stairs to the first floor and said "Linda I am going down to the gas station and buy a lottery ticket be back in a few minutes."

Rob walked out the door and got in the car and drove down to the gas station and bought a lottery ticket. He walked over to the counter to scratch off the numbers on the ticket. He scratched all the numbers except for one. He got to the last one and scratched that.

It said 20 times. Rob scratched the prize off and it said 1 million dollars.

Rob got all excited. He picked up his ticket got in his car and drove home.

"Life will be great now, we will have money" said Rob.

Rob got home and went into the house and said "Linda, get on the computer and find where the nearest lottery office is so we can claim our prize. Linda do it now!"

"How much did we win?" asked Linda

"Millions" said Robby

"No shit" said Linda

"No shit" said Robby, "Get on the computer and find out where the lottery office is and what time they open."

"Let me see the ticket" said Linda

"Here you go" Said Robby

Linda got on the computer and got the address of the lottery office.

"Road trip!" said Robby

Linda and Robby got in the car and drove to the lottery office and claimed their prize.

"How much after taxes?" Robby asked the clerk behind the desk at the lottery office.

"About 15 or 16 million said the clerk, it takes about 3 to 5 weeks and you will get a certified check by registered mail.

"Thank you" said Robby

Linda and Robby left the office ecstatic, happy, feeling financially secure for the first time in their marriage.

As Linda and Robby drove home, Robby said, "We ought to take this award letter home and put it in the strong box so nothing happens to it."

"That's a good idea" said Linda

They went home and put the letter in the strong box.

"Robert", said Linda, "we need some things from the store, we need to go John's discount store, I need to pick a few things up."

"OK" said Robby, "on the way home we will stop and get some lunch."

As Linda and Robby drove to the store, they talked about how good things would be. About how they would help their children, pay off all their bills, take a vacation and put some money in a trust fund for the grandchildren.

"Life will be good," said Linda

"Sure will" said Robby

They pulled in the lot of the store.

As Linda and Robby looked for a parking space, Robby notice a group of men and women standing by a big van carrying weapons.

"That's odd Linda," said Robby, "do you see those men and women with weapons over there standing by that van?"

Linda said, "don't worry about it, probably just military people on their lunch break."

"Your probably right," said Robby.

As Linda and Robby walked into the store, Robby said to Linda, "I have to go to the pharmacy and pick up my prescription where are you going to be?"

She said, "Well I have to get a couple things, I'll meet you at the car."

"OK" said Robby as he walked away from his wife and went down by the pharmacy to pick up his prescription.

"$59" said the pharmacist

Robby gave her his card and picked up the prescription. As he was walking away from the pharmacy he noticed the men and women in military uniforms walk in the door. And they started shooting, shooting at the customers. Rob knew this wasn't right. He was by the bathroom doors so he ducked into the men's bathroom. When Robby went into the bathroom he saw a black man coming out of the stall.

"What the hell's going on out there?" Said the black man

"I don't know," said Robby, "people came in in uniform and started shooting at the customers."

People are screaming, people begging for their lives.

"Don't kill me"

"Don't kill me"

pop pop pop Automatic rifle fire.

The smell of gun powder was in the air strong for what seemed like several minutes

Then they heard a man say, "You three go down to the pharmacy grab all the narcotics and antibiotics out of the pharmacy and then kill all the pharmacists."

"Islam forever! Kill all the infidiles!"

Robby turned on his phone and dialed 911

"Your emergency please?" said the operator.

"I'm at John's discount store and some terrorists came in and started killing the customers and robbing the pharmacy. People are getting killed. Send some help fast!" said Robby.

"What is your name?" the black man asked Robby.

"Robby," said Robby.

"My name is Lou, what are we going to do?"

"Unless you have a couple of AK47's in your pocket I aint gonna do a damn thing but stay here and say out of the way." Said Robby

"My wife is out there!" said Robby to Lou, "Hope she's alright, I pray to God she's alright."

"I came to buy some ribs and food for my wedding reception tomorrow, Tomorrow I'm supposed to be getting married." Said Lou

"Well Lou I haven't heard any gun fire for a while," said Rob,

They slowly and carefully looked out the door of the bathroom. They didn't see anybody with any guns. There were dead bodies and blood but no gunmen. They carefully worked their way towards the front of the store. They heard gun fire coming from the front of the store, It was coming from outside.

As they walked towards the front of the store the gun fire stopped.

"Wonder what that means," said Robby

"I don't know," said Lou

All of the sudden a lot of men came in to the front of the store. Carrying guns, some wore police uniforms, some wore military uniforms.

"Freeze" said a deep voice.

Robby and Lou raised their hands

"Don't shoot, don't shoot!"

"Lay down on the floor face down and put your hands out where I can see them," said the police officer.

Robby and Lou laid down on the floor with their hands out.

"Don't shoot man, don't shoot."

"Who are you guys?" said the police officer.

In the meantime a couple of military officers came up.

"Let's see your ID's," said the soldier.

Robby and Lou took out their ID's and gave them to the police officer.

"What went on in here?" asked the police officer

Robby and Lou said "we don't know, we were in the bathroom and all of the sudden we heard a bunch of shooting. Somebody shouted Islam forever, kill the infidels Then there was a bunch of shooting and yelling and screaming and people begging for their lives. It was horrible all kinds of bodies and blood all over the place."

"My wife is in here someplace," said Robby, "I don't know if she's dead or alive. I'd like to look for my wife I know she's in here someplace."

"Give them back their ID's," said the soldier to the police officer. "See if you can help him find his wife."

"You come with me," said the soldier to Lou.

Lou went with the soldier.

The police officer went with Robby

"I don't know where she is," said Robby, "let's check at the cashier first."

As they walked by the cashier, Robby thought he saw his wife.

"That's not her," he said

"That's not her," he said

Robby saw his wife. He went up to her. She was breathing. "She's alive!" said Robby to the police officer, "get some medical help in here now!"

Police officer got on the radio and said, "get some medical help in here immediately. Get all the medical help in here."

There was a dead woman's body laying on top of Linda. Robby pushed the dead woman's body away.

"Linda can you hear me, Linda can you hear me?" he said

"Yea, I can hear you but I sure am in a lot of pain. I think I lost a lot of blood." Linda said.

"Hang in there Linda, medical help is on the way." Robby looked up, military and police personnel all over the store, checking for survivors.

An Army medic walked up.

"Here she is," said Robby

The army medic walked over to Linda and took her pulse and said, "she's alive."

"How do you feel?" Said the medic to Linda

"Not so good," said Linda, "I feel weak and light headed."

The army medic said, "you've lost a lot of blood but you'll be alright."

A couple minutes later two men came in with a stretcher.

The army medic said, "We are going to put you on a stretcher and get you to the hospital. Just try to stay calm. We're gonna medivac all the wounded to the nearest hospital."

The medic packed the wounds to stop the bleeding.

They put Linda on a stretcher and the two men carried her out the door.

As they carried Linda out the door, Robby held Linda's hand.

"You'll be alright Linda, You'll be alright," said Robby.

As they walked out of the store, it looked like a combat zone, dead bodies inside, dead bodies outside. There was blood all over the ground outside.

Many soldiers, police officers and ambulances outside. The smell of gun powder was heavy in the air.

There was an APA news van with a woman broadcasting the news and camera men.

They took Linda to a helicopter, they put Linda on a helicopter. Robby got in with her. There were other people on the helicopter. The helicopter took off for the hospital.

On the helicopter on the way to the hospital, Robby heard one soldier say to another soldier,

"Just got word that this is happening in 10 other John's stores in 10 different states. The president has declared Marshall law."

The helicopter landed at the hospital. The army medics unloaded the wounded and took them into the emergency room. There was a lot of activity with the doctors and nurses in the emergency room. The army medic told Robby to have a seat it's gonna be a while.

Robby sat down in the waiting room, TV was on.

News commentator said, "It has come over the AP, 10 different stores in 10 different states were attacked by terrorists today. It's estimated thousands have been injured in the attacks. The president of the United States will come on and speak to America in about 20 minutes."

As Robby sat and listened to the news he got on his phone and dialed his son's number. Phone rang.

"Hello"

"Hello Josh it's dad, your mother is at the hospital in Newport News she's been shot. A bunch of terrorists attacked the John's discount store. A bunch of people have been shot and your mother is wounded." said Robby.

Josh says "yea the bases are all on high alert."

"What's it mean Josh?" asked Robby

"I don't know," said Josh, "could be war I don't know. I have to have special permission to leave the base. What hospital are you at?"

"I'm at Newport News Medical center, get back to me when you can come or if you can't come. Mom is ok, she is wounded but she will be ok," said Robby.

Robby hung up his phone and the president came on TV.

"Today America was attacked by terrorists, killed thousands and injured thousands of Americans. I have ordered all military personnel on high alert. I have ordered all reservists be called to active duty and report to their duty station. I called an emergency session of congress, I have declared Marshall law. All airports, train stations and bus stations have been shut down. Flights coming in will be allowed to land but no flights will be allowed to take off. If you don't need to be on the road stay home. We need to get medical personnel to their jobs and military personnel to the bases. I have ordered a nationwide curfew, no one will be allowed after dark until sunrise, with the exception of medical personnel trying to get to work and military personnel trying to get to their base. Anyone caught out after dark that does not fall into that category will have their ID checked and possibly arrested. By executive order I have put a freeze on gasoline prices and other commodities sold to the public. Any gas station or business caught price gouging will be shut down and their business licenses taken away and they will be prosecuted.

I ask the American public to keep their wits about them, be aware of what is going on around them. If you see anything or hear anything that looks suspicious, call the FBI immediately.

God bless and protect America. Thank you."

Robby's phone rang, "Hello," he said.

"Dad what's going on?" said Marie

"Oh Hi Marie." said Robby

"Josh called me and told me that mom has been shot. What the hell is going on?" said Marie

"Well we were at John's discount department store and some terrorists came in and started shooting and killing people. They bought your mother to the hospital, she is being treated by the doctors now. They said she will probably be alright. Hold on a minute." Said Robby.

The doctor approached Robby, "Your wife is ok, she just came out of surgery, she'll be ok. She is in recovery now. They are going to put her in a room. She will probably be here for a few days." Said the doctor.

"Thank you doctor," said Robby, "Did you hear that Marie?"

"Yea I heard, should we come down?" Marie said.

Robby said, "I don't know how you're going to get here, they have shut down all the trains and planes and busses. If you can get here fine, if you can't I will keep you informed."

"OK dad bye." Said Marie

"Bye Marie." Said Robby

Robby hung up from Marie and tried to call Josh again.

"Hello"

"Hi, Josh are you allowed to leave the base and come to the hospital?" asked Robby.

"No," said Josh, "no one is allowed on or off the base until further notice. We are on high alert. There is talk there might be war. The Army has issued fire arms to all personnel on the base. I don't know what is going to happen dad. I don't know when I will get home again. How's mom?"

"She's ok Josh. The doctor came out and said she's out of surgery and she will be in recovery and they will put her in a room and she will be here for a few days. I talked to your sister Marie. The President came on TV and said that they are shutting down all the buses and train stations, they are letting all the busses and trains come in but they are not letting anyone leave. The president said there is a curfew between dark and sunrise, anybody that was on the roads would have their vehicles checked and searched. So I don't know if I will be able to get home tonight." Said Robby.

"OK dad" said Josh.

"OK Josh bye" said Robby

Robby walked outside to grab a cigarette and sit there. He said a prayer, God help us. God help us all. Please watch over my family. As Robby smoked a cigarette, more helicopters were coming in with more wounded. Robby smoked a cigarette and went back in the hospital.

He heard on the PA Robby come to the nurse's desk. Robby went to the nurse's desk and said "my name is Robby."

"Your wife is out of recovery and she is in a room if you want to go see here." Said the nurse.

"What room is she in?" asked Robby.

"410" said the nurse.

Robby walked up to room 410. He walked in the room, Linda was laying in the bed, she was awake but kinda groggy.

"How you doing?" asked Robby.

"OK I guess, kinda hurt a lot." Said Linda

Robby said to Linda, "God has blessed us again a lot of people did not survive that attack."

"I know" said Linda.

Robby turned on the TV and a news commentator came on and they were showing pictures of the store. The military was carrying body bags with bodies in them out of the store and putting them on a truck.

"Wow it's really bad. I talked to Josh and Marie. Josh said they will probably declare war. He said all the bases are on lock down. The army has issued weapons to all personnel on the base. The president has ordered Marshall law and a curfew from dusk to dawn. I don't know if I will be able to get home tonight or not." Said Robby.

"I'm so tired I can barely keep my eyes open." Said Linda, then Linda went to sleep.

Robby was hungry and needed a cigarette so he went down to the cafeteria. Just as he was getting up the press secretary came on TV in a news conference.

A reporter asked, "Are we at war? "

Not at this time. The president is meeting with his cabinet and military leaders. Congress is in an emergency session. I'll get back to you on that. There will be mail delivery as usual starting tomorrow."

Another reporter asked, "How long will Marshall law last?"

"As long as is necessary. The president has ordered all diplomatic personnel and their staff and American citizens to leave the middle eastern countries immediately."

Another reporter asked, "What has been done to contact the next of kin of the dead and injured?"

 "Temporary morgues have been set up for the dead and they are in the process of identifying the dead and injured so we can contact the next of kin. We are working as fast as we can to notify the next of kin."

"After almost an 800 point drop in the stock market the stock market has suspended trade until further notice."

"That's all for now we will get back to you when we know more." Thank you. Said the press secretary.

The press secretary walked away from the podium.

Robby got up from his chair and walked down to the cafeteria and got some food and some coffee. Sat down and ate his food and drank his coffee. He walked outside of the hospital and there were two soldiers standing there with automatic weapons. Rob walked out and stood by the door and smoked a cigarette.

One of the soldiers said, "Good evening sir."

Robby said, "Good evening." Robby smoked a cigarette.

One of the soldiers said, "You have got to stay here tonight it's already starting to get dark."

Robby said, "I know, I know."

Robby walked back into the hospital walked up to his wife's room and sat in the chair. Drank his coffee and relaxed and watched the news.

The news anchor woman came on and said, "The MLB have suspended all games until further notice."

The next morning Robby woke up and looked outside. He looked over at Linda's bed and Josh was sitting there holding his mother's hand.

"Josh" said Robby.

"Hi dad how ya doin?" said Josh.

"I don't know son how are we doing?" said Robby.

"I got permission from the commanding officer to be on duty at the hospital until further notice so I can be near mom." Said Josh.

"That's good son." Said Robby.

"Did you eat? ask Josh.

"Yea son I did, but I could sure use some coffee." Said Robby.

Josh said, "Why don't' you go home and take your medication, I know you didn't take your medication all day yesterday and get back before it gets dark so you can spend time with mom while I'm on guard duty."

"OK son," said Robby.

Robby walked over and gave Josh a hug and kissed his wife.

"Dad," said Josh, "I have made arrangements with Pvt Miller to take you to get your car at John's store. He's waiting for you in the hospital cafeteria. You can't miss him he's a big dude with blonde hair and is wearing his uniform with his name on it."

Robby walked out of his wife's room and walked down to the cafeteria and met Pvt. Miller and introduced himself. Private Miller and Robby walked out of the hospital to Private Millers Army vehicle.

As Robby and Private Miller drove, Private Miller said, "I will follow you home and make sure you get home alright."

As they pulled into the store parking lot, Robby could see chaos in the parking lot. Private Miller dropped Robby off at his car and followed Robby home. When Robby got home and parked his car, he walked up to Private Miller and shook his hand and said "Thank you I appreciate it good luck to you young man."

Robby went into the house and took a shower and changed his clothes and took his pills and sat down and watched TV.

"There have been 750,000 applications to carry firearms since the terrorist attack. The lines at the gas stations are 5-10 miles long. The Governors of each state have spotters out looking for price gougers at gas stations and stores. Grocery stores are running out of food." said the news anchor.

The phone rang and it was Josh.

"Dad, I got a loaded 45 in the plastic dresser in my exercise room, keep it handy don't carry it on you though because they will arrest you for carrying a loaded weapon without a license. Keep it handy in case there is any trouble at home." said Josh.

"OK son," said Robby, "How's your mother doing?"

"She's ok she's awake. We've been talking. I go on duty pretty soon." Said Josh.

"Ok Josh, I'm gonna get something to eat really quick and then I'm going to come back to the hospital." said Robby.

"OK dad."

"Bye Josh"

"Bye dad"

Rob finished his food, gathered his pills and walked out of the apartment.

Rob walked out the front door with his change of clothes and his pills. He went out to his car and got in his car. Two men pull up behind his car.

"Where ya going man?" said one of the men.

"I'm going to see my wife in the hospital, she was shot in the raid at the store." Said Robby.

"You live in this complex?" one man said.

"I sure do! You know me I'm Josh's father." Said Robby.

Another man in the cart said, "Yea that's Josh's father he's ok."

"What's going on?" Robby asked.

"There have been armed bandits doing home invasions. Stealing food, drugs, money and anything else they can steal," said one man. "You need proof you live here to get back in. The complex has armed guards at the front of the complex and armed guards patrolling the complex 24 hours a day."

Then the man handed Robby a tag and said, "Wear this when you're in the complex so we know you're a resident. Any looters or home invaders will be shot on sight."

"OK" said Robby

The men pulled away and Robby went and sat on the stoop of his townhouse and called his son.

"Hello"

"Hello Josh it's dad, I just heard there were armed men going around doing home invasions. Stealing people's food, money, drugs and anything they can take," said Robby.

Josh said, "I know I saw it on the news. A lot of cases they are killing the occupants of the houses. I suggest you stay at home."

"OK son, who's gonna watch your mother?" said Robby.

"When I'm not on guard duty I'll stay with her. I'll let you know when it's safe to leave," said Josh.

"OK son," said Robby, "Let me talk to your mother."

"I'm on guard duty now as soon as I get off guard duty I tell her you need to talk to her," said Josh.

Robby said, "Has she got her phone?"

"I think so" said Josh

"OK I'll just call her phone," said Robby.

Robby hung up from Josh and called his wife's phone number.

"Hello"

"Hi Linda how ya doing?" said Robby

"I'm doing ok, still got some pain," said Linda.

"I want to come see you but Josh said there are armed bandits out there robbing and killing people. He told me I should stay home and he will come and see you when he's not on guard duty," said Robby.

"OK honey you take care of yourself, keep in touch," said Linda.

"OK honey I love you," said Robby.

"Love you too honey bye bye," said Linda.

Robby went into the house and got his sons loaded 45 and his radio and went outside on the front stoop and smoked his cigarette. He turned on the radio and the news commentator said day 2 has not gotten any better. The governor has declared the state in a state of emergency and closed the schools and state offices. Robby sat back and smoked his cigarette and heard the news commentator say the governor will speak to the public in about 10 minutes. Robby took his radio and his sons 45 and went in the house. He turned the TV on and sat down. He kept the 45 on the couch next to him.

The governor came on TV

"It has come to our attention that a bands of armed men are approaching citizens at stop lights and stop signs and robbing and murdering them. Stay home if you don't have to go somewhere. If you are not Police or military personnel or medical personnel stay home. We have state police patrolling streets and highways. There have been several gun fights insued between state police, metro police and these bands. Some band members have been shot and killed. I am in the process of making arrangements with the federal government to have food supplies shipped into our area. As soon as that becomes available I will let the public know and arrange for distribution. If you need help such as ambulance or fire call 911 and we will get to you as soon as we can." Said the governor.

The news commentator came back on and said "We have footage of what's going on in the area, Some of it taken from a helicopter. The footage shows all the businesses the gas stations the grocery stores and so on all displaying signs saying out of stock or closed. People were sitting in front of their businesses with guns guarding their businesses from looters. The footage showed miles of abandon cars by gas stations. The commentator said, "these guys probably didn't get lucky enough to get any gas. The news broadcaster said the president will speak to the public in a half hour."

Robby called his daughter.

"Hello"

"Hi Marie it's dad," said Robby.

"You ok?" asked Marie.

"I'm fine stay home Marie don't go out. Where's Charlie?" asked Robby.

"He's in the kitchen why?" asked Marie.

"Tell him to stay home no job is worth dying for." said Robby.

Marie said, "yea I know we saw on the news that we should stay home they are robbing and shooting people on the streets."

"OK honey stay safe bye bye," said Rob

The news commentator came on and said, "What you're seeing now are cars in the middle of the highway with bodies lying next to them. Victims of armed bandits were attacking motorists and robbing them and murdering them. Again if you don't have to leave your house, don't. Nothing is so important that you have to leave home. If you aren't medical or military or police stay home. I repeat stay home!"

Robby heard a knock at the door. Robby got up and took the chain off the door. Robby opened the door and two men were standing there. Robby held his gun in his hand.

"Easy old timer we are with the FBI and they held up their ID's. I'm agent Murphy and this is agent Johnson. We would like to ask you a few questions." Said one man.

"Come in," said Robby.

The two men came in and sat down.

"We understand you were in the store when it was attacked," said agent Murphy.

"Yes I was," said Robby.

"Can you tell us what you heard or saw?" said agent Murphy.

"Be glad to." said Robby. "I had just left the pharmacy and was heading towards the front of the store and they came in and started shooting and I ducked into the bathroom. There was another man in there and we stayed in there to avoid being shot. Then the shooting stopped. Then we came out and I started heading for the front of the store looking for my wife. Police and Military came in and assisted me in finding my wife and they took her to the helicopter. "

"Did you see or hear anything while you were in the store?" asked agent Johnson.

"Yes, said Robby, when my wife and I first pulled into the lot of the store we saw men and women in uniforms carrying weapons standing by a van.

While we were in the bathroom we heard a man say Kill the Infidiles Islam will live forever." Said Robby, "You two guys go down to the pharmacy and get all the narcotics and anti biotics and kill the pharmacists. Then we heard some more shooting. After a few minutes the shooting stopped. Lou and I carefully left the bathroom and walked towards the front of the store. A police officer approached us and checked our IDs. Lou went with one of the soldiers and the police officer helped me find my wife and we called the paramedic and she was then taken to the hospital. What the hell is going on? Said Robby

As the FBI men and Robby sat and talked the news commentator came on and said, "The president will be on shortly."

Agent Murphy said, "Do you mind if we sit here and watch this?"

Robby said "No, you are more than welcome to. Would you like a cup of coffee or a beverage or something to eat."

They both said no thank you

The president came on and said:

"Good morning Americans to date I have news about those involved in the raids on John's store have been either arrested or killed. We have also arrested and are questioning over 400 individuals who are thought to be connected with the raids. All these individuals had student ID's from colleges local to the John's stores and are all here in the US with student visas. All are citizens of Muslim nations. Surviving terrorists and individuals involved in these attacks have been arrested and will be treated with the same compassion and dignity as the terrorists showed the victims of the John's store attacks. I have issued an executive order that all postal carriers be issued permission to carry firearms and be issued fire arms and told to use those as necessary to protect themselves and US mail. I have spoken to all the governors of the states, and told them that gasoline supplies, food supplies, medicines and other essentials are on their way to all the states. And the state and local governments will distribute the supplies as they see fit and based on need. I have asked congress to reinstate the draft and any individuals between the age of 18 and 35 years old that are not full time high school students or full time college students that have not maintained a B average or higher will not be given deferments. This will mean that those eligible for the draft will be sent to military training camps.

They will receive military training and be put on reserve status and be sent home until such time as the nation needs their service."

A man approached the president as he stood at the podium speaking and handed the president a piece of paper.

The president spoke again, "I have just been informed of the count of dead and wounded. There are 12,000 dead this figure would include customers killed in the raid, law personnel and military personnel killed during the raid. There were another 3,000 injured and taken to hospitals. We do not have a count of motorists killed or wounded and individuals killed or wounded during home invasions. Again this includes customers, law personnel and military personnel.

Our hearts and prayers go out to all the relatives of the dead and wounded and the survivors. I have been informed that the CEO of John's discount store corporation has set up 3 billion dollars in a fund to cover the expenses of the victims of John's discount store raid have incurred. Please do not contact the federal government for these reimbursements. John's discount has set up an 800 number so individuals having a claim can call. Individuals, survivors or families of the dead will be contacted by mail.

I have issued an executive order that all individuals that are not American born citizens or naturalized citizens from Muslim countries be expelled from the US. We have already started seizing bank accounts and real estate and other assets owned by these individuals. I was told by other world leaders and governments that they are doing the same thing. These actions are being taken to insure the safety and security of Americans and people all over the world. Individuals that are American born citizens or naturalized citizens who are not connected to any terrorist group, you have nothing to worry about. Your rights will be protected like any other American citizen by guarantee of the constitution of the US. But if you do have a connection to any terrorist group beware we will come to get you. You will be considered a security risk. I want to assure those individuals that are recipients of SS checks and VA benefit checks and military you will continue to receive your checks without interruption. I ask all Americans to keep your wits about you, look around you, be aware of what is going on around you. If you see or hear anything that looks suspicious contact the FBI.

Thank you. The press secretary will now answer any questions."

The president walked away from the podium and the press secretary came up to the podium.

The press secretary came up to the microphone and said, "We will now take any questions."

One reporter spoke up, "Isn't this thing where we are expelling Muslims from the country a lot like when the government arrested the Japanese in WWII?"

"No," said the press secretary, "again only non-American citizens will be detained and expelled. Those that prove not to be a threat to national security or are tied to any terrorist group will no longer be bothered. Those that prove to be tied to any terrorist group will be expelled from the country. Their property seized, their bank accounts seized. We have to do this to protect our country and our nation and our citizens."

One reporter stands up and says, "This draft where we are drafting men and sending them to boot camp and then sending them home, what is the point of that?"

The press secretary responded, "These men and women that are drafted between the ages of 18 and 30 who are not full time students or have not maintained a B average in college will be sent to boot camp and be given military training and then sent home and be on reserve status and will be called up in the event we need them. If we do not need them they will not be called up."

Another reporter stood up, "What about the dead in the temporary morgues? Have any bodies been claimed by any surviving family members? And how much of that 3 Billion dollars will each family member get?"

"Due to current events it has been difficult for relatives of the victims to identify the dead. IT will be done," Said the press secretary. "As far as how much each family member will get it is between John's club and the surviving family members."

Another reporter stood up, "What is America going to do in retaliation to the attacks on innocent Americans? Have we declared war yet?"

"The president has deployed our military assests to locations we cannot disclose at this time, as well as other nations have deployed their assets to other areas of the world. That best serves the free world and protects American citizens as well as their own citizens. Due to security I cannot say more about that," said the press secretary

One reporter stands up, "The food and gasoline supplies sent to other states, when do you expect them to arrive and how will they be distributed?"

The press secretary responded, "Most of the shortages were created by panic buying after the attack on the John's stores. As far as distribution, there will be a limit of 8 gal per customer of gas and food will be dispensed based on size of the family and your needs. Once again in case anyone has forgotten, any business that is caught price gouging will have their license taken away and be shut down.

That's all for now gentlemen, there will be no more, we will get back to you."

The agent Murphy said, "I think we have all we need now Robby, if we need more information we will be in touch with you."

"I hope I have helped you as much as I can," said Robby.

The FBI walked out the door and Robby walked out the door behind them and sat down on the stoop.

The next morning Robby walked outside and sat down on the stoop and had a cigarette. A lot of people were gathering in the middle of the parking lot. Robby got up off his stoop and walked over to the neighbors, "what is going on?" asked Robby of a couple neighbors he knew.

I was talking to my husband and he was told they are going to lift the lock down on the base. Open up the commissary and PX again sometime soon," Said one neighbor.

One female neighbor asked, "you know I'm 25 years old does that mean I am going to get drafted like the president said?"

Robby said, "I don't know."

Another neighbor said, "I don't know, my wife is in the Army, we have two kids, your guess is as good as mine. You don't think they will take both parents do you?"

The other neighbor said, "I don't know. We will have to find out."

There was a radio playing in the background and a news reporter came on and said the governor will speak in a few minutes. Everyone sat quietly and they turned the sound up so they could hear it.

Good afternoon citizens, I am pleased to report that for the most part the roving gangs that were robbing and murdering citizens in their cars and homes have been killed off or arrested. Those that haven't been caught have slithered back under the rocks that they came from. Everything is now safe although proceed with caution, you can go back on the streets. Local, county and state police will continue to patrol the streets to make sure there is no danger.

A loud cheer went out amongst the neighbors.

One neighbor said, "I haven't had a cigarette for a day and a half, I'm dying for a cigarette. Another one said I'm almost out of food, I'm already into my hurricane emergency supply."

Another neighbor said, "I don't know if I'm going to go anywhere I'm out of gas, I'm on E."

One of the neighbors was a pastor at a local church. He said, "The churches in the area have contacted each other and are going to work together to help the locals as soon as we can."

The news broadcaster came on the radio again and everybody got quiet. The news commentator said, "It has come from the White House that as of 8 AM tomorrow Marshall law will be lifted the lock down on the bases will be lifted. Maybe life in America will get back to normal. God Bless America and Americans."

The news commentator went on to say "As of 8 AM tomorrow airports, train stations and bus stations will be allowed to operate once more. If you are not already at the airport or train station or bus station, don't come unless you are picking up passengers. Those passengers at these conveniences will be allowed to continue on their trip, be allowed to return to their homes 48 hours from tomorrow morning those public conveniences will once again start making reservations and accepting passengers."

A cheer came up from the crowd.

A white car approached the crowd. They were employees of the complex, they said, "Effective 8 o'clock tomorrow when the Marshall law is lifted, we will remove the barricades from the complex and the armed guards will be removed. The armed guard patrols will be discontinued. However we will continue to have a 24 hour patrol of the complex for a couple more days." They went on to say, "If you see or hear anything suspicious, after you have called the local authorities, please come to the complex office let us know so we can look into it. God bless you all."

One neighbor asked the man, "Should we continue to wear our tags?"

"I would suggest it, at least for the next two or three days. After that there probably won't be a need to," the man said.

Robby asked if there would be a problem if he wanted to go visit his wife at the hospital if there would be a problem getting out of the complex and getting back in again.

He said, "There shouldn't be a problem, just make sure you are wearing your tag and your picture ID so you can get out and get back in."

Robby walked away from the crowd, walked into his apt and put away his son's gun and extra ammunition, picked up his car keys, and went out to his car and drove up to the gate. There were two men standing there with guns at a barricade. Robby stopped. One man says "let's see your ID and tag."

Robby showed them his ID and his tag.

"OK go ahead, don't forget to get back in you have to show your ID and tag to show you're a resident."

"OK" said Robby.

The man walked up to the car and moved the barricade and Robby pulled out and headed for the hospital.

As Robby drove to the hospital with his spirits up he saw a lot of tow trucks along the way picking up abandon cars. He looked at his gas gauge; Thank God we bought gas before all this happened. He had a full tank of gas.

Robby got to the hospital and there were two armed guards standing at the entrance to the hospital.

"ID please and state your business."

"My wife is here, she was shot at the John's club store, I'm here to see her, here's my ID." Robby showed his driver's license and his military ID.

"OK Go ahead."

Robby drove in the lot and parked his car, he was all excited he was going to see his wife for the first time in a while. While walking in the hospital there were two armed guards standing there. He walked in and the guards asked Robby for his ID. Robby showed them his ID. State your business said the guard.

"I am here to see my wife Linda she was shot at the John's discount store during the raid," said Robby.

"OK go ahead check in at the nurse's desk."

Robby walked in and went up to the nurse's desk and identified himself and showed his ID and his military ID.

The guard at the station said, "go ahead sir."

Robby walked into his wife's room and Linda was laying there and the nurse was changing her bandage. He saw Josh sitting in a chair holding his weapon. Robby walked in and hugged his son Josh.

"What a mess huh Josh?" said Robby.

"Yea dad," said Josh.

The nurse finished changing Linda's dressing and Robby walked up and gave his wife a big kiss and hug.

"I missed you honey I really did," said Robby.

"I missed you too Robby." said Linda.

"How you feeling?" asked Robby.

"I'm ok, Dr. tells me I'll be able to go home in a few days, won't be able to do too much but I will be able to go home. I have to take some antibiotics and he's going to give me some pain pills. But I will be able to come home," said Linda

"That's great," said Robby.

"You know what Robby?" said Linda, "With the exception of when Josh had guard duty he's been with me every minute of the day, I have my own body guard."

"That's good," said Robby to Linda, " it's been a hell of a mess out there. People have been getting killed in their cars so forth. Did you tell Josh the good news yet Linda?"

"What news is that?" asked Linda.

"About the lottery," said Robby.

"Oh" said Linda.

Linda turned and said, "Josh we won 20 million dollars in an instant lottery ticket the day this mess started. We should get a check in the next 3 to 5 weeks for 15 million dollars."

Robby says, "I'm hungry I forgot to eat today."

Linda said, "Let me call the nurse."

She called the nurse and the nurse came in the room and Linda asked, "Is it possible to get a sandwich for my husband?"

"Well we are kinda short of food but we will see if we can't scare up a sandwich and a cup of coffee for him," said the nurse.

"Thank you," said Linda.

Robby said, "You know God has blessed us again."

Josh said, "You know dad I know I told you I was an atheist and didn't believe in God but I got to be honest with you I prayed a couple of times since this all started."

"Good," said Robby.

"Excellent!" said Linda, "We will convert you to Christianity yet."

"Josh," said Robby, "Every morning I pray to God and thank him for the many blessings that he has shown to our family. And I ask him to continue to watch over our family."

Linda asked Josh, "Do you think we will go to war?"

"I don't know mom but I'm at my current duty station for at least another year and a half and hopefully by then this mess will be over," said Josh.

Ten days later

Robby and his family sat in the living room eating their lunch and watching TV and the show was interrupted by the president of the United States.

"I received word today that thousands of people were dying every day in the Muslim countries of an unknown disease. All the nations of the world have been asked to send medical personnel and medicines to the region. We have also heard from Russia and China and they are going to send medicine and doctors. I have talked to the leaders of our allies and we have come to the conclusion that we are not going to risk our nations citizens by exposing them to the disease. I have ordered that military to stop all ships and airplanes to the Muslim nations and Russia and China and we are not allowing entry to our ports and airports from these nations. We refuse to expose our citizens to this disease. The only reason we are including Russia and China is because they are helping these countries and we don't want them bringing the disease over here. After talking to our allies we have all concluded that this is God's way of ridding the world of terrorists and murders. We don't want to interfere with Gods work.

God bless American citizens and citizens in the nations of our allies.

Thank you."

This is dedicated to the men women and children that have been murdered by terrorists around the world in the past those that will be killed in the future. God bless us all.

THE END

The brick

Be a character in the story.
LIST OF STORY CHARACTERS

Jess

Larry

Donna

Uncle Mike

Debbie

Emma

Doctor

Nurse

All Their Lives Were Changed When They Came Together Due to circumstances Beyond Their Control.

THE BRICK

It was a cold and very windy day. A storm was brewing the waves and surf were rough and high

Jess and Donna sat on a bench on the beach. As they conversed about a little of everything, when Donna noticed a lot of bright red brick like objects coming in with the tide. Donna & jess walked to the water edge to investigate the red objects. They seemed to give off a warm burst of air. They almost seemed to be breathing with a slight movement. Jess suggested they call someone.

"Who do you have in mind?" Asked Donna

"I'm not sure" answered Jess.

"Have you noticed the air is getting warmer?" Donna reached down and held her hand a few inches above one of the red objects. It was radiating warm air.

"Check this out." said Donna.

Jess held his hand just above one of the objects.

"It feels like a banked campfire." stated Jess. "Let's call Larry and have him bring his metal milk containers to transport some of these objects home for more study."

By the time Larry arrived the temperature by the beach got so warm Jess and Donna had to take off their winter coats.

"There must be a 40 to 50 degree difference in temperature between the beach and the parking lot." stated Larry as he removed his winter coat. "I'll back the truck up. We'll put one object in each container. Here put on these gloves to protect your hands."

As the three worked quickly picking up the objects and putting them in the milk containers, the three sweat. Their shirts were soaked from the heat off the objects. Picking up all of the objects and loading the containers on the truck.

"Look at the containers." said Jess, "Do you see the heat rise from them?"

Jess put his hand close to ta container, from 10 inches away, it started to burn his hand. Jess and Donna followed Larry to his farm. On the way to Larry's farm, Larry called his uncle and told him to meet them there. Larry's uncle is a mechanical engineer.

When Jess and Donna and Larry arrived at the farm, Larry's uncle was waiting for them. His uncle Mike greeted Larry.

"What do you have there?" asked Uncle Mike.

"We're not sure but they put out a lot of heat." answered Larry.

Mike approached the truck and when he was about two feet from the truck, it was almost too hot to get any closer.

The four quickly unloaded the containers and put them in a covered but open shed. Again the winter temp went up 50 to 60 degrees. The four soaked with sweat from handling the containers. They were a little apprehensive as to what they were dealing with.

"You know, we might have a inexhaustible fuel, it could replace oil as a source of energy. Come with me." stated Mike. "I have an idea."

All four of them went into Larry's workshop. Larry called his wife on his workshop phone extension and told her to bring out some lemonade. She did. "Larry, why is there lightning over and around the open shed?" asked his wife.

All four went outside to see the lightning. The temperature outside was like August. It was December. It began to rain. It was like a warm summer rain.

Larry told his wife to make coffee and sandwiches and keep them coming. "Donna will give you a hand. Us men are going to find a marketable use for our discovery."

They worked all night eating while working. Come sunrise they men finished building a working prototype furnace using one of the brick like objects only. Mike calculated the furnace could heat the average size house for some time maybe even years. After the men took time to eat breakfast, they did a visual check on the other brick like objects. There was no temperature change of the objects and no difference in their appearance. As the men sat in fron of the workshop, drinking coffee, Larry's daughter pulled in the driveway. Larry walked up to her car and greeted her. She saids confused "About five miles from here it's close to zero temperature with snow and freezing rain and turned to 80 degrees almost immediately. I get here and it's 80 degrees here. What's going on?"

The men looked at each other.

"What do you make of it Mike?" asked Jess.

Maybe the objects could be used to control the weather? We need to have three people drive in the remaining three directions to see just how much of the area the warm temperature covers. We also need to find out how many objects it takes to maintain the tropical weather."

The women were sent in three different directions to check it out. When they returned they reported for five miles in each direction the weather was tropic. They all stood in a group talking excitedly about the new discovery. "The possibilities were endless." Declares Mike with great enthusiasm. "We can make fossil fuels worthless. I'm thinking our brick objects could power an automobile and if we use your old pickup truck, convert it to brick power."

"it'll work? Said Jess to Larry. " What do you all think?"

They all agreed.

"I'll draw some plans to do so." Jess, Larry you two start to work removing the engine and drive train from the truck. Don't throw any parts away. Be careful not to damage the electrical systems and wires. We can re-use them. As well as the brake systems and the suspension systems. Don't remove the radiator until we know if we can use it or not. Take off the gas tank clean it as best you can. Best there's no trace of gas in it. Larry doesn't your daughter work for a patent attorney?"

"Yes" said Larry.

Jess and Larry told their wives to drive back to the beach to see if there are more brick objects.

"If there are call and let us know and we'll get some more milk cans and pick them up. Larry have your daughter call her boss and tell him we need to see him as soon as possible. Don't tell him any more than you have to. OK?

Mike went to work drawing up plans. Larry and Jess started dismantling the truck. The two wives drove to the beach. A half hour later the wives called. There were more red bricks on the beach. They also said there were some people on the beach watching the red bricks come in with the tide. More are afraid than curious.

"Get here quick!"

Jess and Larry left straight away for the beach. Picking up some milk cans along the way. When Jess and Larry arrived at the beach, there was a small crowd of people all of them had removed their winter clothes. Larry backed the truck up to the beach while they got the people to move out of the way he told them they were from the EPA sent to remove the red bricks for the public's safety, to Jess and Larry's surprise they believed them.

Larry, Jess and their wives set to picking up the red bricks. They didn't need all the cans they brought. After loading all the cans on the truck, they left the beach. As they pulled out of the beach parking lot, four police cars pulled into the lot. Larry, Jess and their wives left the area hoping no one got their license plate number. When they arrived home the men set up a canvas canopy to cover the new cans. Mike came out of the workshop, "I've finished the plans for our brick drive. We might have some minor changes as we work, maybe not. First thing we have to do is prepare the truck for modifications."

As the men worked on the truck using some old parts from the truck, and some newly made parts, the women kept the sandwiches and coffee coming. Larry's daughter told the men her boss said he'd be at the farm tomorrow morning with the necessary documents to apply for a patent. After many hours working on the truck, the men were ready to test the truck.

Except for a very few minor problems they test went well. After making more heat units in the brick storage space they were ready to run a second test. The control test went perfect. The electric power test went perfect. The brake system went perfect. All that remained was the forward and reverse test and steering test and speed control test. Mike was the test driver Jess went along to take notes on the test drive. After a rough start and getting used to the controls the test went well. After returning from the test run, both Mike and Jess were very excited everything went well.

"We might have to revert some pressure from the brake lines, other than that we have created a hot air powered auto." said Mike.

All the men and women were ecstatic with their success after a minor change in the brake system a second test run was made. They reached speeds of sixty five miles per hour with more power to spare. The adjustment on the brake system resolved that problem. After returning from the second test and learning the news the six hugged each other and laughed and cheered. They broke out some champagne and toasted each other.

Mike said "Before we get to loaded we need to open the heat release valves."

Mike did that, he also showed all of them how to use all the different controls. Then they celebrated in earnest late into the night.

The next morning they talked over their next step. While eating breakfast they all agreed before anything else patents had to be filed. Secondly, form a charter S corporation. After accepting these things they looked into new uses for the bricks. The possibilities were endless. Now with the exception of minor aches and pains all six of them were fairly healthy. All of them wore glasses. Mike crowding eighty had full upper and lower dentures. Jess, Donna, Larry and his wife Emma were in their mid-sixty's having partial dentures. Larry's daughter Debbie being forty five, like Donna and Emma had already been through and finished menopause. They three men had gray hair as well, being partially bald. Donna and Emma had all gray hair. Debbie was showing some gray hair. Not knowing who they could trust, over the following two weeks, they from time to time visited the question of should they and if so who to tell about their discovery.

A few days later they felt totally exhausted unable to stay awake. They thought they might be dying. They went to their beds and fell into a deep sleep.

Was this their end?

Debbie opened her eyes. She felt great! Better than she had in years, but confused. She knew she was in the hospital. She didn't know why. Over the next few moments the other five woke up. They all wanted to know why they were in the hospital. They felt great.

Donna said, "it's dark outside and there is frost on the windows."

"I don't have my glasses on but I can see like I do." stated Mike.

The other five said the same.

"I don't have my hearing aid on and my hearing is perfect" Said Emma.

"That's nothing," declared Mike, "I have a mouth full of teeth and it's not my dentures."

"I don't know about you two guys but I've got a chubby I could use to know down a large tree." stated Larry with a big smile on his face.

Emma walked over to Larry's bed.

"Let me see." She said.

After he showed her, her eyes opened wide, her mouth fell open.

"Thant could definitely knock down a tree." Emma stated with a smile on her face. Mike and Jess said they also could knock down a few trees too.

"Show me." said Donna to Jess.

After looking she said, "Maybe a whole forest. With your long black wavy hair you look like you did when I married you forty years ago."

"It would seem none of us have gray hair anymore and the three of us men have a full head of hair." All of them agreed.

Jess pushed the nurses call button. When the nurse came in she demanded they all get back into bed.

"You're sick," she said.

"lady we all feel great, like we're forty years old again. Bring on some food and coffee and be quick about it." ordered Donna.

"Oh my, oh my" the nurse said confused and a little intimidated. "I'm getting the doctor let him deal with you people."

As she ran out of the room, the six conversed excitedly about their rejuvenation and maybe finding a cure for old age.

After a few minutes they nurse brought in six trays of food.

"We're starting you out on a soft food diet until we can be sure it's safe for you to have a regular diet," said the nurse. "The doctor will be in in an hour or so."

"Soft diet my butt!" said Mike. "Bring some food we can sink our teeth into and take this garbage away."

Once again the nurse ran from the room, again intimidated and a little frightened.

One at a time the six took a shower. Like the men, the women were pleased with their body's improvements.

Debbie stated her breasts were a little tender and felt a little heavy. Other than that, she felt great. Emma replied, "If I didn't know better I'd say you're pregnant."

"No way! Said Debbie, "It's been over a year since I, you know."

A half hour or so later the doctor and a man in a suit came into the room. Behind the doctor, came in the nurse keeping her distance from the patients.

"Good morning how are we all doing today?" asked the doctor.

"We all feel like a million bucks" they replied, "We're hungry for some real food and when do we get out of here?"

"I'm Dr. Jeffery's and you people have got to stop scaring my nurses please. I'll see you get food you can sink your teeth into, but stop scaring my nurses. I am concerned that you want all your food raw or uncooked including the meat."

"We apologize for that." Stated Mike "but we feel very healthy and hungry. We also wanna know how long we've been here and why are we here?"

"You were brought here almost two months ago unresponsive in a comatose state. We weren't sure if you were going to live or not. You're all very healthy now and beyond my understanding in physical condition of people a third your ages" explained the doctor. "Maybe you can enlighten me how."

"You wouldn't believe us if we told you." They answered.

"Nurse, take their vitals and see they get regular diet food and they've assured me they won't scare you anymore."

"Allow me to introduce inspector Robert Williams with the FBI to you. Folks if you will be kind enough to answer his questions maybe we can get you out of here and send you home. Thank you."

'Debbie our test show your three months pregnant. "

"No way can't be, I've not you know, for over a year," stated Debbie worried and confused. "My breasts are tender and feel a little heavy but I don't feel pregnant."

We can run another test but I'm sure your tender breasts and heaviness is because your pregnant, said the doctor.

Debbie became frightened and angry. How could this be?

Good morning, I have just a few questions, it will only take a few minutes, stated the inspector.

They doctor took a seat. He wasn't missing this for anything.

How do you explain being bald, gray haired and have no teeth? Just plain old when you were brought in two months ago and the body's changes that took place over that two months. The doctor waited with great curiosity to hear the answer.

Inspector, do you like hot dogs? If you do, do you enjoy eating them or do you ask what's in them? asked Jess.

If you shared your secret it could benefit millions, said the doctor, a little disappointed.

We don't have a problem helping mankind, we do have a problem letting the government get control of it and making it financially out of reach of those who need it.

Their food is here doctor, said the nurse.

I won't allow them to eat until they answer my questions. Take it away, said the inspector.

I don't think so, said the doctor, very angry. How dare you treat my patients so, bring the food in now and leave. I won't have my patients abused, not even by the federal government!

I will not leave, stated the inspector, angrily. If necessary I will put them in protective custody, taking them out of your jurisdiction. Take the food away nurse.

Bring the food in immediately! Stated the doctor as he picked up the phone and called security. Send all security staff to ward 2B stat! Lock down status!

As the patients watched the war of wills between the doctor and inspector, they decided to trust the doctor with their secrets. Moments later, they security came on the ward. This man is endangering my patients, it's my medical diagnoses he be held for observation on the phsyc ward as prescribed by state law for no less than thirty days. To keep him from using phones or the internet to threaten others he is to have neither phone nor internet privileges. All visitors he might have must be supervised by a security staff member.

You can't hold me against my will! I'll sue! The inspector declared reaching for his gun

Stop him he's going for a gun! ordered the doctor. Put him in one of the padded rooms. You security staff are witnesses he is a threat to himself and others. Take him away now.

After the inspector had been removed by security, Jess said, you in trouble for sure now doctor. We all agree to share our secrets with you. It's time for a road trip. You will see for yourself why, how and the results we'd tell you, but you would never believe it in a million years.

The patients began to applaud the doctor.

You are truly a humanitarian.

You all know we're all going to be considered criminals from here on, said the doctor.

If it be a crime to help mankind, let us make the most of it, declared Larry with pride and vigor.

Here, here the other five chanted.

All the patients hurried and got dressed. Doctor and all the patients left the ward and hospital and headed for Larry's farm.

As the doctor's van entered the tropical area the doctor started asking a lot of questions.

When last at the farm there was a fifteen mile wide and of tropic weather around the farm.

If you'll just be patient all your questions will be answered, said Donna.

Doctor how do you explain me being pregnant? I swear it's been over a year since I, you know, I'm totally confused and a little afraid, Said Debbie.

When I get a handle on what's happening on the farm, I'm hopeful I'll be able to give you some answers. In the meantime, try not to stress over it, it's not good for the baby, answered the doctor.

If I didn't know better I'd swear we are being followed said Jess with concern.

They all turned to see if they were being followed.

I believe your right.

It's too small of a car so it probably not the FBI or police.

Slow down see if they pass us, answered Mike.

The car didn't pass, it slowed down to pull over and stop.

See what happened? said Larry.

They did. The car following them did the same.

There's only one person in the car, said Mike.

All the men left the van and walked to the car following them. The driver's window went down.

Dude, why are you following us? Aren't you the nurse on ward 2B? asked Jess. "Yes" she replied.

Why are you following us? The doctor asked.

Doctor I don't know what is going on but I find myself wanting to be a part of it she said with hope in her eyes. I am a nurse and for once I'd want to be part of a monumental moment in mankind.

Debbie being pregnant might just need me. Please doctor let me join your

It's up to you gentlemen, what do you say? asked the doctor.

We trust you what do you say doctor? They replied.

Please doctor, all I want to do is help, the nurse replied.

Ok nurse you're in.

Be aware, there will be a lot unknown things happen. I can't guarantee your life or health. If you're still interested leave your car and join us in the van quickly. stated the doctor.

Yes sir, replied the nurse. Doctor I brought some supplies we could use. They are in the trunk, Julie stated.

She walked to the trunk and opened it. The doctor looked in the trunk.

On second thought, we don't have room in the van for the supplies so you follow us in your car and thank you, good thinking, he said smiling.

I'll ride with her so she doesn't get lost, volunteered Mike.

With that they continued on their journey. Mike and Julie had a friendly and informative talk. Julie couldn't believe what Mike told her. She kept saying "that's almost unbelievable."

Mike told her, we will be there shortly, and seeing is believing, as he gave her a big smile. The two became good friends. Upon their arrival, they exited the vehicles. It seems to me the temperature has gone up about ten or fifteen degrees since we were here last, commented Mike. After checking the thermometer on the house, they became concerned. As natural temperatures rose so did the tropical temperature around the farm. The temperature at and around the farm could become fatal to man in the near future.

Doctor, at what point do temperatures become dangerous to man?

I'm just guessing, but when natural temperatures reach eighty degrees or above your probably going to see the farm and the tropical area around the farm becomes uninhabitable. The tropic climate will be very hot and may be deadly, said the doctor. I suggest we convert the doctor and nurse's cars to hot air power. Take the pickup truck and move on. When we're out of the area, we'll call the government and let them deal with the situation. Of course, we'll leave behind the remaining fifty four objects.

Take ten brick objects with us to do experiments on.

All in favor, asked Mike?

They all agreed and set to work converting the vehicles. Being as hot as it was, frequent water breaks were necessary. By the end of the fifth day, they'd converted the vehicles to hot air power. Which was good, considering the temperature at the farm had reached one hundred and thirty degrees. It was getting difficult to breath for the doctor and nurse. The original six had no problem breathing but were uncomfortable in the heat.

After quickly loading food and water supplies in the vehicles they left as soon as possible.

Hot air could be seen rising from the ground. They drove non-stop for some time. Once again the doctor and nurse could breathe without difficulty. When they came to a roadside restaurant, they stopped for a meal and called the government. They stayed on the phone long enough to give the location of the farm and warn them of the harsh temperatures and then hung up.

They still didn't know where the brick objects came from.

Are they a living thing or a strange source of energy? Do they reproduce and if so how?

How long do they continue to give off warm air?

How did they rejuvenate Mike Jess, Donna, Larry, Emma and Debbie and how did Debbie become pregnant?

Was it by touching one of the brick objects?

What will her offspring look like?

How did they change the original six to be able to tolerate extreme heat and does it apply to extreme cold?

Are the red brick objects a blessing to mankind or a curse on mankind?

Only time will tell.

THE END

The Chair

Be A Character In The Story

List Of Story Characters

Waitress
Lovely Young Woman
Chair

Love Story

THE CHAIR

BY

RICHARD G. SWEITZER

She was young, blonde and beautiful, with everything to live for. Being warm and friendly, people took to her naturally. She came into my life on a cold December day at a holiday party.

You see, as I bathed for my date, I prayed, "God, send me someone to call my own." As it were, my planned date stood me up.

Seeing as I had already paid for the tickets, I was determined to get my money's worth, so I went to the party alone. Seated at the table were six others, one of which was her. She had a nice smile, great knockers and butt. What was not to like? We didn't say too much to each other at first. The waitress began serving the meal. After everybody was served at the table, I told the waitress, "You forgot my date's meal."

She replied, "sir nobody is sitting in that chair."

Having had a few drinks I replied, "You don't see this luscious creature sitting there?"

"Sir the chair is empty." Exclaimed the waitress slightly baffled.

"Waitress, I suggest you stop hurting my date's feelings and bring her dinner. After all just because she is real thin is no reason to make her feel bad. So bring her dinner now."

The waitress brought her dinner.

At that point I realized the whole table was cracking up with laughter and I joined in. The young woman and I emphasize young, introduced herself and so did I.

As the evening progressed, we got to know each other better. We talked, danced, and laughed a lot and a little sparking. We spent the next three days enjoying each other's company. After dating for a few months, we got engaged and within a year we married.

She was nineteen years old, I was 29 years old.

To date, we are married just shy of forty years and still in love.

The chair is no longer empty.

Comments From Readers

"I Couldn't Put it Down"

"Great Endings"

"I liked it"

"Shocking"

"Exciting"

"I liked it so much I read it twice."